Contents

About the author

Sue Bannister believes anything is possible, despite having dyslexia; for her it's the right mindset that counts.

Her early memories of crewing a Cadet sailing dinghy at the age of five, at Hayling Island Sailing Club, are of exhilaration – a simultaneous mix of nerves, tension and great excitement.

Sailing quickly became a passion and part of her DNA, spending her childhood around boats, bobbing about the Solent in a yacht on the south coast of England with her parents, two sisters and Ollie the dog.

Thanks to Sue's early years of mucking around in boats, she blossomed into an experienced racing sailor, competing in sailing championships at local, national and world level. She has been the first lady President of the UK Flying Fifteen Association and now enjoys retirement with her husband sailing their Dehler 37 yacht. Volunteering as a qualified coach at Thursday Club, an initiative at Hayling Island Sailing Club that helps children from the local community to get out on the water, is among her favourite pastimes.

The idea for a childrens' boating story has been a few years in the making and has now arrived in print, sharing with readers Sue's love of having fun in boats. Her other passion is skiing, so perhaps a ski adventure book is on the cards…

"Rope's Off on the High Seas" is Sue's second book. She has previously published "No Sugar My Journey My Choice", a biography about her recovery from primary and secondary cancer.

Introduction

This story is all about Rope, and how with the helping hands of Sheet, Halyard and Bosun, he falls in love with sailing.

He wants to become a champion, but decides to become a confident sailor first.

In this tale you'll meet Sheet, who is Rope's big sister; then there is Halyard, his older brother and Rope is the youngest.

In the coming pages, you'll find out how the holiday is made rather special by their godfather Bosun, with whom they love spending their summer. You will see how he guides and encourages them to fully appreciate the fine art of bobbing about on the water.

Let's start with Rope. Full of energy, he loves to do things – not necessarily in the right order, because things just happen around him. Until now, Rope has never been sailing, but this is soon to change.

9

Halyard, on the other hand, is already a bit of an old sea dog. Older than Rope, he is accomplished in both the art of sailing and paddle-boarding. Paddle-boarding is a sport where you travel across water, or ride the waves, on a specially made buoyant board. You can sit, kneel or stand to paddle it. For those who have never seen a paddle-board, it is a similar shape to an ironing board without legs, but a bit longer and thicker.

As we start our story, Halyard's preference is for paddle-boarding over sailing. It gives him great opportunity to combine his love of fresh air with vigorous exercise. At the moment he knows little about racing sailboats, but he plans to learn more during the summer. He loves his sister and his brother and he really enjoys helping others.

Sheet is the boys' elder sister and sailing is always her first choice. She is a true natural around boats. As you read on, you'll see that Sheet's ability to learn quickly is thanks to the way she listens carefully *before* diving in head first. It works well and gets her great results.

Halyard and Rope, on the other hand, are not patient enough to take that approach and just works things out as they go. Sheet has adapted a little boat named 'Come Alongside' to be either a sail boat or a row boat, depending on the weather.

Let's set the scene. Both Halyard and Sheet have pets – Half-Hitch, an English bulldog, belongs to Halyard, and Painter is Sheet's friendly cat. Rope doesn't really have a pet, but he decides it might be a nice idea to adopt one during the summer.

Their pets play a big part in the childrens' adventure with Bosun. Halyard's dog brings some of its own challenges; he is not the ideal pet for someone whose passion is spending time on the water. This is because English bulldogs do not float – it is true that they have zero bouyancy. But Halyard works round this by playing safe, and making sure that Half-Hitch wears his lifejacket before heading anywhere near the water.

Half-Hitch absolutely adores Halyard and never misses a trip that involves water – wetter the better, it seems – even for a dog that cannot swim. You will find out more about Half-Hitch in the coming pages.

Then there is Painter, Sheet's cat. She can swim and thoroughly enjoys dipping her paws in the water as Sheet sails along. Sometimes she can be easily startled, but  not when she is onboard Sheet's little boat 'Come Alongside'. She either curls up in the bow, or goes on lookout, giving the impression that she's helping Sheet find her way! More than likely, she's hoping for a fish or two.

Although Rope's main quest this summer is to learn to sail, he also wants to adopt a pet. But what kind of pet? He'd like one that costs nothing to feed and one that doesn't need to be taken for a walk each day. A pet without costs and without a lot of responsibility would be the best of both worlds, thinks Rope. Over the course of the next weeks, he soon discovers that adopting his pet comes with its own hiccups. Was it a price worth paying? Maybe!

Remember, throughout their adventures the children are watched over by Rope and Halyard's godfather, Bosun. How cool is that!

Bosun is an early riser. Fishing is one of his rituals and he loves the quietness of early morning before breakfast. He heads out to cast his line without too many distractions.

But Painter, Sheet's cat, knows all about fishing too and is quick to get in on the act. The minute Bosun picks up his fishing rod, Painter is first to the door, with an ever hopeful look in her eyes as she gazes up at him. Painter comes back after many a trip licking her paws. You may be wondering why?

Fortunately for Bosun, he has an ideal job which allows him to do something he loves and has also earned him the nickname 'Bosun'. In case you've not come across one before, a bosun's job is to look after boats. Wherever there are boats and ships you'll find a bosun, hard at work in a workshop, repairing and maintaining all kinds of craft. A bosun is also an able seaman, who can handle sail boats, dinghies, motor yachts, launches and all kinds of craft out on the water as well as in the workshop.

In our story, while Bosun works in his workshop, he's just a stone's throw from the Boat-House and the Boat-Park is only 20 metres away. It is all conveniently placed so that he can keep a watchful eye on the three children as he works.

Let's begin

The Boat-House, Boat-Shed and Boat-Park

The Harbour

If you look carefully The Boat-House, Boat-Shed and Boat-Park are tucked on the south east bank of the harbour.

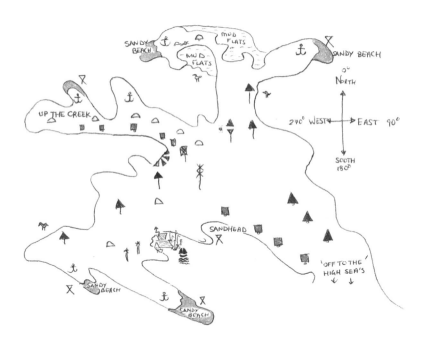

This is the little boat Rope is using

Below are a few boat names.

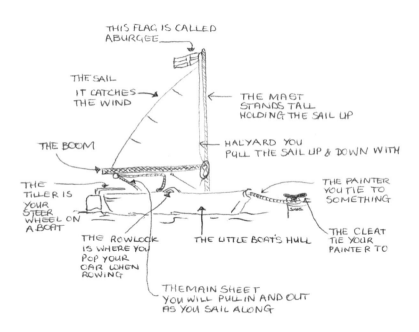

THIS FLAG IS CALLED A BURGEE

THE SAIL IT CATCHES THE WIND

THE MAST STANDS TALL HOLDING THE SAIL UP

THE BOOM

HALYARD YOU PULL THE SAIL UP & DOWN WITH

THE TILLER IS YOUR STEER WHEEL ON A BOAT

THE PAINTER YOU TIE TO SOMETHING

THE ROWLOCK IS WHERE YOU POP YOUR OAR WHEN ROWING

THE LITTLE BOAT'S HULL

THE CLEAT TIE YOUR PAINTER TO

THE MAIN SHEET YOU WILL PULL IN AND OUT AS YOU SAIL ALONG

1

Hold the stick - oops the tiller

It's the second day of his summer holiday and Rope's taking forever to eat breakfast. Slowly chewing his cereal, he rewinds the events of two days ago in his mind. Today could have been so different...

It was at home, two nights ago, that Rope had watched his Dad hastily packing his work bag, following a phone call that had summoned him immediately back to his ship.

Hot on the heels of that first blow, Mum had told the three children that unfortunately, plans for their normal family summer holiday would have to be cancelled. "Grandma is too frail to be left alone and with Dad back on the ship, there's no option for us to go away now. I *am* sorry."

It was like the sun going out for Sheet, Halyard and Rope. Suddenly there were no plans for their summer holiday. Their faces fell and their hearts were heavy.

Having anticipated their disappointment and sensing, after her announcement, just how crestfallen the children were, their mother had gone straight to the phone. She had called Bosun.

Rope remembers how he had listened to her side of the conversation with baited breath, wishing all the while that recent events were just a dream.

"Bosun!" – Mum never called him by his real name – "How are you? So sorry it's rather late. I'm afraid we have a problem and I'll have to cancel."

Rope had listened miserably while she explained the details of what had happened and how she wished it didn't have to be this way. "Inner city London in the summer is no place for anyone – let alone three very excited children who've already packed their bags over a week ago. And Rope was so looking forward to going sailing for the first time!"

Then Mum had stopped speaking as she listened to Bosun's reply.

Rope had been on tenterhooks watching her expressions, trying to guess what Bosun was saying. Mum had nodded her head every so often, shaken it once or twice. Rope had been on the edge of his chair until, after what seemed a lifetime, he had heard her say,

"You're right! Sheet is 16… so technically she's old enough to keep an eye on both boys and with you acting *in loco parentis*, Bosun, things would work fine."

Then more silence this end, as Bosun continued the conversation.

"Wow! Are you *sure?*" Mum had suddenly sounded really excited. "Of course, you're godfather to two of them, but all *three* – really?!"

Nobody breathed. You could have heard a pin drop.

"OK, fantastic! I'll drop them off tomorrow as planned and I'll call you each evening for an update. Bosun, the children will be thrilled! That's so kind. Thank you – how can I ever repay you?! I'll come down as soon as…"

At that point Rope had stopped listening. All he could think was that everything was going to be fine after all.

Then yesterday, when their mother had dropped them outside the Boat-House down on the south coast, she had given the three of them big hugs all round.

"Stop fussing, mum," Sheet had said. "We'll be fine and the boys will be as good as gold." As she said that, Sheet shot the boys one of her looks that left them no room for doubt – they would be good as gold.

Rope remembers how he and Halyard had nodded in agreement, making their best efforts to look reassuring. And the rest is history, thinks Rope as he returns to the present, still munching his cereal and trying to guess which boat he will be going out in today. He stares out of the window in the direction of the Boat-Park, wondering.

Just why he is making such a meal of breakfast is probably because he has the biggest smile beaming across his face as well as butterflies in his tummy from all the excitement. And all because this is the day he is going sailing for the first time. It has all been arranged by Bosun. Sheet has kindly agreed to take him out, immediately after breakfast, in the little boat 'Come Alongside'.

Rope pictures his first voyage out on the high seas in a little boat with his big sis. A voyage! On the high seas! At home, he watches so many films and his imagination is so vivid that it takes him to some wonderful places. Maybe in a previous life he was an explorer? But then he thinks perphaps 'the high seas' might be a bit of an exaggeration for today's adventure – oh well…

Next he remembers the words his brother and sister always use when they talk about boating. It sounds like a completely foreign language to him. They say things like "pull the halyard." How odd, he thinks, to be pulling my brother. "Lee ho!"

Hmmm, haven't met him yet. "Ready about!" Not really sure about that one either. Eager not be confused by the terminology, Rope is confident that today's outing in the little sailboat will change all that.

Soon Rope can't contain his excitement any longer. Pushing away his half eaten cereal, he jumps up from the table, leaving the remains of the meal to clear up later. He feels sure he will be forgiven for the mess, today of all days, and runs upstairs to get ready, bumping into Sheet on the way.

"What's the hurry?" Sheet asks him, not expecting an answer and not receiving one either.

Breathless, Rope arrives in his bedroom to find a mass of sailing clothes and gear spread carefully across the spare bed. Bosun had set it all out much earlier, while Rope slept, and has thoughtfully left a list of instructions, item by item, to help Rope put it all on in the right order.

On looking he discovers there is a pair of sailing shoes; some funny looking fingerless gloves, sun block cream, a pair of wrap round sunglasses, a sunhat, a lightweight spray top with a front pocket, a pair of swim shorts, and rash vest, a towel and a lifejacket with front zip that fastens with velcro straps.

As soon as he's dressed, Rope rushes downstairs, bursting to see the boat, and heads to the backdoor. But Sheet stops him in his tracks. "Let me tidy you up," she says. "Wait a mo if it is ok with you, I am just off to get the boat ready myself. We could go together if you like?"

"Great!" says Rope.

Sheet straightens Rope's lifejacket and they both head for the Boat-Park. Rope talks incessantly, questions coming thick and fast.

"How fast will it go? Will I get wet? I can't wait to see the boat!"

Sheet prepares 'Come Alongside' for the water, but Rope is too excited to watch everything she is doing and he only catches snippets of what she is saying. He almost feels as if he isn't really there, and is watching it all from far away.

Just as the boat's ready to go down to the water, Bosun arrives to help them push the trolley. After the launch, Bosun pulls the trolley back up the beach again, away from the edge of the sea and Rope notices a big red ribbon on it.

That's strange, thinks Rope. "Why the ribbon?" he asks, but nobody has time to reply.

Down at the boat, Rope perches on the side of the deck. It's all wobbly! This is his first experience of floating on a boat on the water. Even with Sheet holding the little boat it still wobbles. It's a really funny feeling! Rope's smile widens and he wonders what will happen next? He sees Sheet fiddling with something before she climbs aboard.

Rope's is so happy and he feels himself drifting away in a daydream. Sheet loves it when Rope does that. Moments before she gives the boat its final push off, she points at Rope. No response. She tries again, nudging him this time. "Please hold the tiller firm," she says.

Rope is suddenly alert. The tiller, she had said. He tries to fathom what and where the tiller is? And why does he need to hold it firm? A confused look flits across his face. Sheet smiles and point to a stick just behind him.

"Ah! *that's* the tiller!"

"It's that stick at the back of the boat," explains Sheet. "It'll wobble around if you don't hold it firm."

Rope grabs it and holds on.

Sheet finally pushes them off. She pulls herself onboard, splashing Rope in the process and nestles in beside him for his first ever sail. Neither of them spot Bosun waving as he walks up the beach. They are far too busy looking around the boat.

Mesmerised by the motion of the boat, Rope continues to grasp the tiller, unaware that he is actually in charge of the boat. 'Come Alongside' heads out from shore on a straight course, bobbing over the water. Echoes of laughter from the boat reach Bosun, as he watches Rope pointing at different bits of the boat.

Still at the tiller, Rope's confidence grows as they sail further away from shore, but he can hear his heart pounding and his head is full of questions. "What is the tiller attached to?" "What should I do next?" "Why do I need to hold the tiller anyway?" "Did I hear right that the tiller can also be called the helm?"

There's so much to take in and he doesn't want to miss anything. Neither does he want to distract Sheet. He just wants to soak up every little thing there is to know about sailing! So Rope decides to save the questions for later. And for once, he does exactly as he is asked!

He is also really keen to please his sis. He is seeing another side of her now than he usually sees, and it's a side he likes even more. At the same time that Rope is thinking these thoughts, Sheet is realising that Rope's character onboard is different to *his* normal nature too. He is very obedient, he is happy to do as she asks, without actually understanding why. He's listening intently, absorbing everything he is told. Smiling all the time, he is trying to make sense of his first sailboat outing.

Rope reflects on the first moment after Sheet pushed the boat off, and how odd it is that he can feel all the movement of the boat through his body as he holds the stick in his hand. The little craft continues to bob gently as they sail further from shore.

For a minute, Sheet forgets that Rope has absolutely no idea how to sail, until they narrowly miss another boat by a whisker. But thanks to her quick reactions, she nudges Rope's hand to make 'Come Alongside' change course and fortunately they avoid a collision.

"Bit of a close shave, but we have a clear passage ahead now," she says.

Sheet encourages Rope to give a wider berth to passing boats from now on. Rope doesn't actually know what she means by the term 'berth', but he pretends to and nods his head anyway.

Meanwhile Rope cannot fathom why his sister is not holding the stick… er tiller, but he does notice that the butterflies in his tummy have quietened down a lot, even after that near miss. Is he heading in the right direction? He's still not sure, but he continues to obey Sheet's commands and holds the tiller firm to keep the boat on course!

Sheet is mindful that Rope is prone to daydreams and keeps a watchful eye for the telltale signs. All is fine for the moment; she adjust the sails and they sail gently onward. The air is warm and scented with the salty fragrance of the sea. The clear water fizzes past the stern of the boat. After a while, a light breeze fills in and the boat tilts over a little.

Sheet hears Rope say "Aye Aye, Cap'n!" and she wonders whether he is off on another imaginary trip of his own. Then she sees Rope's knuckles – white from the effort of holding the tiller firm.

"Lightly as you do it" she tells him. "Have you seen your fingers?"

Rope glances behind him and is surprised to see how tightly he is grasping the tiller. Sheet senses that this is a good time for her to take the helm herself. She moves carefully around and prizes the tiller from her brother's clenched hand. The boat responds to the change at the helm by tipping a little, then settles again as Sheet takes control.

Now Rope is sitting in front of Sheet, smiling his wide smile and wiggling his fingers to get the circulation flowing in them again. From his new position, he has a clearer view of what is ahead and begins to relax.

Sheet knows his fingers will be fine and continues to point out lots of other interesting things that you might be lucky enough to see on a boat trip: for a fleeting second they see the sleek head of a seal break the surface just in front of them.

At that moment, Rope has a brainwave! Unable to contain himself, he blurts out his idea. "I'm going to have a pet. Well, not a *real* pet, but I'm going to adopt that seal. D'you know what I'm going to call it? Sammy!"

Sheet laughs. "A fine idea indeed." Soon afterwards, she asks Rope to pull something in. Unsure, Rope asks what she means. She calmly asks "can you pull the blue sheet in a couple of centimetres? It will help us go faster."

Rope is all for going faster. He looks around for something resembling a blue sheet, then remembers that 'sheet' is a boating term for a rope that controls the sails. He pulls it in and feels the wind blowing faster past his ears.

"If I pull it in some more, will we go even faster?" he wants to know. Sheet giggles and shakes her head.

Rope decides he must tell Bosun there's a lot to do when

sailing, pulling this and that in and out… His thoughts drift and he contemplates how lovely it would be to be able to get around the harbour as confidently as Sheet can when she sails 'Come Alongside'. He hopes he'll be able to if he spends the rest of the holiday on the water. The idea of sailing on his own takes root in his mind – it's something he really wants.

He thinks about what he has already learnt today. What happens if you hold the helm too tightly? He wiggles his fingers some more, because they still look a bit on the white-side. And what happens when you sail in different directions? Rope now knows that you have to change sides in the boat, but only after Sheet has called "ready about!" and "Lee ho!" Still not quite sure about Lee ho because he hasn't met him yet – it'll probably all come clear when he's sailed a bit more.

He discovers too, that the Skipper is the person who holds the stick… tiller… helm. And he is so grateful that Sheet took the tiller from him half way through. Based on today's sail, he prefers pulling the sheets to taking the tiller. But the names in sailing are so confusing – being asked to pull a line that has the same name as his sis, whatever next?!

Sheet decides it's high time they head back to shore. "Ready about?' she calls.

"Ready!" answers Rope.

"Undo the sheet – let it go – Lee ho!" In the excitement of changing sides in the boat and getting everything right, Rope peers round, still confused by the call "Lee Ho." Is he looking for the wrong thing? The beach looms ahead. "Let off the green sheet – it will slow us down before we hit the shore," Sheet explains. "And be ready to pull up the centreboard fully!"

As Rope feels the thrill of the shore fast approaching for the first time, he forgets his recent instructions on what and how much to pull up and when to jump out. He waits for his next instruction, as they stand, ready to jump from the boat. At a prompt from Sheet, Rope jumps straight overboard, but misses his footing as 'Come Alongside' thumps to an abrupt halt, running aground into the sandy bottom. Rope flies headlong into the water with a mighty splash! And all because the centreboard had only been pulled half up…

Meanwhile, Bosun and Halyard, up by the Boat-Shed, hear commotion from the water's edge. They turn and see a splashing heap in the water, at first not realising it is Rope. Halyard welcomes the disruption and giggles, once he realises the heap is Rope.

Rope is not fazed by being dumped in the sea. He shakes himself off and smiles at Sheet. "And for my next trick?"

Sheet tries to look serious, but fails. Laughing, she sends him for the trolley. "Remember, it's the one with the red ribbon on it."

Rope looks up the beach to where a mass of near-identical trollies are crowded together. He spots theirs immediately and returns to the edge of the sea with it, leaving a trail of water dripping behind him.

"That ribbon's definitely a good idea. I see why you have one after all" he says.

"All credit to Bosun – it's his idea," replies Sheet. "Now I'll show you how we get the boat back on the trolley without lifting her."

Rope watches as Sheet pushes 'Come Alongside' back into the water a little until she re-floats, clear of the sandy bottom. The trolley slips easily underneath the hull, so that the boat can be pulled slowly out of the water. Tying the boat to the trolley stops her falling off as it is towed away from the water and up the beach.

"Why do you call the boat a 'her' and not a 'him'?" asks Rope.

"Good question – all boats are 'she' or 'her'," replies Sheet.

29

Together they pull 'Come
Alongside' up on to the beach
just above the water line, where
they roll up the sails neatly. Back
at the Boat-Park, Sheet hoses down
the boat with fresh water to clean
off all the salt, then pulls
the boat cover
on. "Almost
finished!" she
announces.

Meanwhile Rope is chattering and asking questions, fumbling with a piece of string at the same time. After a few seconds, during which his head is full of images of Halyard's dog at the same time as he tries to remember a knot demonstration that Sheet gave earlier, he asks

"Is this how to tie a Half-Hitch?"

Sheet looks up from fastening the boat cover to see Rope proudly showing her a perfect Half-Hitch knot. She is delighted and pleased that he's such an enthusiastic fast learner. "Well done you!"

"There's still so much I want to know!" says Rope.

"We'll make a sailor of you yet, but first we need you out of those wet clothes," says his sister, patting him on the back in delight as they head to the Boat-House.

As they walk together, Rope's head is bursting with thoughts and ideas. He can't wait to tell his brother how much fun he's had in the boat today. Maybe Bosun might know if there's a sailing course for beginners any time soon? In his excitement, Rope walks faster and faster until he's almost running, leaving Sheet far behind.

Once in the Boat-House, Rope's straight upstairs to get dried and changed, then straight downstairs again, eager and ready for Bosun's arrival. Meanwhile Sheet is at the kettle, brewing a cup of tea, one for her and one for Rope. Tea after sailing is one of Sheet's rituals.

"It'll go down even better with a biscuit," she says, handing a cup to Rope. Rope passes the biscuit tin to Sheet.

"You choose first."

"Ah… a jammy dodger – my favourite! Just what I need. Thanks."

"And thank *you* for a great day, Sheet. Have another one – you deserve it after such a great time boating," replies Rope.

"Pleasure's all mine," smiles Sheet, taking another biscuit. "I had lots of fun – you should be thanking Bosun for the idea."

"Oh, I *will*," says Rope.

Then Sheet tells Rope what Bosun had said to her when she first started sailing. "He said, when you become a competent sailor, Sheet, you can pick your own little boat to use whenever you're down here. And he even let me name her."

"How cool is that!" thinks Rope.

"And don't forget you have some news to share about your new adopted pet," she reminds him.

Rope remembers Bosun's words to Sheet. Need to become a competent sailor first. That sounds right up his own street, and he can't wait to chat with Bosun. Then, just like magic, in walk Bosun and Halyard.

"How was it?" asks Bosun.

Breathlessly, Rope tells him, "I've adopted a pet called Sammy and my knuckles went white – look! We almost hit a boat and I went flying into the water! I really love it!" He pours a squash for them both, asking "Is there a beginners' sailing course I could go on, one starting soon? I'd love to go on one please."

"Actually there is, but I need to check something first and I'll let you know." Bosun turns and heads back out without touching his glass of squash. Half an hour later he's back with good news.

"As I thought! We've had a cancellation on the course, which means there is a place for you if you'd like it?"

"Oh, yes *please*." He hugs Bosun.

"Alright – early supper for you Rope. You've a busy week ahead."

Halyard joins in "You want to be your best for the start of the course tomorrow, don't you Rope?"

"Tomorrow – oh yes, I do!"

That evening in the Boat-House, Rope had no time for chatter – he was completely absorbed in a pile of sailing books for beginners reading all about tacking. He believes that tacking while reading this chapter is – changing sides as the boat swings through the wind. Got it! Convincing himself, that moving from one side to the other side will help him on the course, he is one minute on one sofa, then off and onto the other sofa, the next.

"Why on earth are you doing that?" his older siblings want to know.

"It'll help me to be ready when they call 'Ready About' tomorrow."

They watch Rope in disbelief, wondering what he'll do next. After half an hour of sofa tacking, he's off upstairs to inspect the kit that's been put out for his course next day. A big sail bag sits at the end of his bed. Next thing they hear is a whistle being blown.

"A whistle – wonderful! and some bits of string. I can tie these together – wow! Perfect." Rope lies back, happy, resting on his pillow and thinks about tomorrow.

The others stay downstairs until they're sure Rope has tucked himself up in bed. They know he usually settles quickly if left to his own devices.

When they creep upstairs, they find Rope sound asleep, a whistle in one hand and a book drooping from the other. Sheet carefully disengages the book and the whistle, putting them on the side before she pulls up the duvet, turns out the light and blows him a good night kiss.

That night, Rope dreams he's aboard a Tall Ship, on watch on a stormy night. The Captain has told him to sound the alarm by blowing his whistle if oncoming boats come close by. Later, he is startled awake by the sound of a whistle, to discover it's already morning. That was a good dream... and today he starts his course!

He is first downstairs every morning that week. He soon falls into a routine. All day on the water, back at the Boat-House soaked to the skin each evening, a quick wash and change into dry clothes, before joining the others for tea. Each evening, barely drawing breath, Rope treats the others to a blow-by-blow account of his day – nothing missed out – before taking himself to bed without being asked to.

On the second night, Sheet offers to test him on points of sail. He jumps at her help.

Rope looks down, then points at the compass, "hmm, did you say 45°?"

"Yes, Rope you might find it easier if you share Halyard's notes."

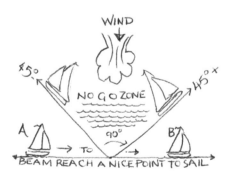

Halyard, meanwhile, is also on a course where he's learning about the finer points of racing.

He's thoroughly enjoying being back in sailing boats again. Now he is learning to read the wind and the tides and he's finding it all fascinating.

Bosun is delighted with both the boys' progress, particularly Rope's ability to have fun doing the capsize drill. He recalls the moment Rope's mast and sail were floating in the water and the boat capsized on its side. Next he dived straight in the water, then swam rapidly around to the other side of the boat, ready to grab the centreboard as he pulled himself up effortlessly onto it. *The next bit you have to see.* Rope pretended he had to walk the *plank backwards*, right up until the boat started to tip towards him, at the same time he swung himself back into the boat as it righted. Safely in the upright boat, without catching a breath, the smile was priceless and his comment too. "That's fun, can I do that again?" Genius *manoeuvre*, if only the other students on the course had the same attitude… it would make it much easier to teach them.

Not surprisingly, Rope passes with flying colours.

2

What's the anchor?

The atmosphere in the Boat-House is positively aglow since Rope passed his sailing course.

Never in his wildest dreams, just one week ago, could he see himself as an able sailor, or sailing a dinghy on his own – let alone passing the sailing course. Now in the second week of his holidays, Rope pinches himself to make sure it's not all a daydream. But it's real, and he smiles, thinking how lucky he is.

Rope wants to thank Sheet and Bosun for their help. But how? He thinks for a bit and decides that first he'll do something for Sheet. His dreams all week have revolved around sailing and eating; snippets of a picnic float into his mind and he decides that a combination of sailing and picnicking could be fun.

So how can he arrange a perfect day for a sailing picnic? Although Rope is famous for running before he can walk, he decides that this idea must be thought out properly. His motto for today is 'planning'.

Rope decides to approach Bosun before he can make any further plans. After all, as things stand he has no boat; no food for a picnic and no idea where to picnic either. He is also very aware, fresh from his sailing course, that the weather conditions need to be perfect. Today, in his opinion, is a perfect day. No time to lose!

To start with, Rope thinks he'll find Bosun straight after breakfast, and he feels sure Bosun will give his picnic plan the thumbs up. Too excited to eat, he pushes his untouched cereal away, thinking he'll come back to it later.

He's halfway across the threshold when his brother Halyard calls out,

"Hold on a minute! What's the hurry? – you haven't touched your cereal."

"I'm going to see Bosun."

"That sounds interesting…"

"I'll tell you later, when I'm back," and with that Rope is out of the back door and away.

Outside, Rope checks his watch. He might still be able to catch Bosun fishing if he's quick, because today's the day Bosun normally goes to get fuel for all the motor launches. Rope finds him exactly where he thought he would – reeling in a fish.

"Supper tonight," smiles Bosun.

"Excellent," replies Rope, and quickly starts explaining all about his picnic day idea, and how he wants to thank Sheet for her help.

"That's a great plan and a kind gesture," Bosun gives him a thumbs up. "I suggest you take the same little boat you used for the course."

"Wonderful! Thanks!"

With that, Rope spins on his heel and heads back to the Boat-House with a spring in his step, ready to share his news with Halyard over breakfast. He arrives back looking rather pleased with himself and is glad to find Halyard alone in the kitchen. With his brother's help, Rope hopes they can create the best surprise ever for Sheet, and all before she is even dressed.

Thrilled, Rope spits out the whole plan. "I had a dream, and yes, Bosun likes it too. He has only gone and agreed that I can use the little boat! So I can have this Picnic Day today! It's my way of thanking Sheet for all she's done in the past two weeks. Oh, and did I say Bosun is letting me use the little boat?"

"Wow, you've been busy," says his brother, indicating that Rope take a seat at the table. "Have some breakfast and we can talk over your plan."

Rope tackles his cereal, and repeats his plan more slowly and calmly this time.

"Great idea, and kind of you to think of it, too. What have you sorted out so far?" asks Halyard.

"Well, it's a picnic and we're going sailing."

"What time will you set out?"

"As soon as we can. About 11 o'clock – that should work with the tides."

"That sounds right. How can I help?"

Before Rope can reply, Halyard speaks again, "I know the harbour really well. How about I go ahead on my paddle-board to find the picnic spot, and before I go, I can check your little boat first. Would that work?"

"Yes, please," nods Rope.

"I can easily take the picnic mat in my water-proof pack and that just leaves you to bring the picnic and Sheet."

"Perfect", agrees Rope.

"I'll see what I can find in the cupboards," adds Halyard.

"Halyard, Bosun suggests that because the tide will be falling, I should anchor off the beach, rather than beach the boat on the shingle. What do you think?"

"Let's do what Bosun suggests – he knows best. And the little boat is a bit heavy for me to drag up the beach."

Rope is not sure that he knows how to anchor off the beach, but decides to put that detail to the back of his mind to think about later. He is sure Halyard will come up trumps when he needs him.

Meanwhile, throughout the boys' discussion, Half-Hitch the dog has been lounging under the breakfast table, without a care in the world. Rope peeps under the table.

"Your dog looks so patient."

"Wait till he sees me with my paddle!"

With breakfast finished and two cups of tea later, the boys are making a final check through the list: landing spot for the picnic – agreed; Halyard is taking the picnic mat, Rope is sorting the picnic, here's the picnic basket, we just need some provisions.

"Don't forget we need to run the idea past Sheet," says Halyard. "I'm sure once she hears your plan, Rope, she'll will want to help in some way too." Rope finds two bags of crisps on the table from last night and puts them in the picnic basket. "All we need now are some drinks and we'll be sorted," he says.

Halyard goes to wash up his breakfast bowl, but Rope says "Leave it – I'll do that when I do mine."

With that, Rope starts opening all the doors in the kitchen, hunting for the dishwasher. "Found it," he says, arriving at the last door on the left.

Halyard is thankful for a few extra minutes to gather his gear. He's noticed how much more helpful Rope is, since his first outing in 'Come Alongside'. And with that thought in his head, he goes upstairs to change.

Sensing an outing, Half-Hitch emerges from under the table and stretches himself out on the floor not far from the back door.

Upstairs on the landing, Halyard crosses paths with Sheet who appears to be heading back into her room. That's odd – she's usually early down to breakfast, he thinks. But he does notice a wide smile spread across her face.

A few minutes later, all togged up in his sailing gear and with the paddle under his arm, Halyard is back downstairs. He tries to step carefully over Half-Hitch. Too late! Rope watches as the dog, who has seen the paddle, leaps up in clumsy welcome, sending a kitchen stool tumbling with his wagging backside as he bolts to the back door, racing Halyard to get out.

The prospect of water! Half-Hitch wags his whole backside in excitement – he doesn't have a tail and often knocks things akimbo before standing, panting, beside the back door. This is the moment that Halyard must fasten the lifejacket around the dog's barrel body, before attending to his own.

"See you later!" calls Halyard grabbing the paddle as he heads out, accompanied by Half-Hitch.

Rope runs over to see them off. "Look out for us – we'll be on the right just past the eighth yellow buoy, on the right hand... er the starboard side!"

"OK!" and with that they were gone.

Rope went back inside, closing the back door behind him. He's very grateful for Halyard's assistance with the plan because it will allow him to concentrate on the sailing element of the trip. If he's to impress Sheet, he really needs to get the sailing just right. He knows that today, the key to the plan working out will be to focus on one thing at a time. Hmmmm... it could be tricky. But he's satisfied with the plan on the whole and begins to clear up the breakfast things, humming to himself as he goes.

At that moment, Sheet appears at the top of the stairs. He can tell she's in a great mood and can't wait to share his surprise.

What Rope hasn't realised is that Sheet, whilst on the landing half an hour earlier, had overheard snippets of the boys' conversation. On hearing the idea, and not wanting to spoil the moment, she had decided to give the boys time to finalise the plans before showing her face downstairs.

Sheet sees that Rope's cleared the breakfast things for him and for Halyard.

"Trying to get in your bro's good books?" she asks.

"It's the least I can do – he's helping out with something," says Rope, keen to spin the secret for as long as he can.

"I get the idea you two are concocting a plan – I'd love to know what is so special about today," says Sheet.

He couldn't ask for a better opening and Rope goes straight into overdrive, talking very fast and launching his plans for the special outing.

"It's a picnic day… Halyard's taking a picnic mat… I'm getting a picnic together," he gabbles, pointing proudly to the basket of provisions he is packing.

"How did you say Halyard's involved?" asks his sister.

"He's gone ahead to check the boats before he finds the perfect spot for the picnic."

"That's kind of him," says Sheet who is secretly pleased to hear that Halyard has agreed to help. Sheet is really looking forward to her treat and to being spoilt and so she decides, at first, not to volunteer to do anything about the arrangements for the trip. But she knows the kind of picnic the boys will put together – a pack of crisps and a tin of drink – and today she fancies something more substantial. So she changes her mind and adds,

"It's so thoughtful of you and Halyard to arrange this for me. Shall I prepare the picnic?"

She suggests Rope goes off to rig up the boat, knowing that Bosun will be there to give a hand.

Rope heads off to clean his teeth and gather the rest of his sailing gear. He leaves the Boat-House in record time, happy with his plan.

Looking forward to the prospect of the picnic day, Sheet calls after him that she'll be there with the picnic basket as soon as she's packed it. "Do I have time to bake a few things?"

"We're aiming to leave the beach at 11 o'clock – is that enough time?" asks Rope.

Sheet puts on her apron and starts to bake some goodies for the picnic basket.

Rope stops for a moment outside the Boat-House, reminding himself that his intention today is to show Sheet how much he appreciates her help and to practice what he's learnt since passing the course. The boat needs to look spit-spot ready for her arrival. He strides off.

A bit later on, Rope is standing back, considering the boat. Is everything right? Has he rigged it correctly? Satisfied that all is in order, he sits on the sand to wait for Sheet. Within a few minutes, his sister arrives, skipping towards him and swinging the picnic basket.

That looks quite full, thinks Rope as he studies the basket, and it smells deliciously of freshly baked pies!

Meanwhile, in the Boat-Shed, Bosun sees Sheet walk past, prompting him to down tools so that he can check over the boat before they set sail. "I'll pull the trolley back up the beach for you if you like, when you're both ready to go?" he suggests and gives the boat a thorough, but surreptitious check, without Rope noticing.

Rope is so pleased – all is going to plan. He steadies the boat by holding the painter – a small piece of rope tied to the bow – while Sheet stows the picnic onboard. Sheet is also giving everything a sneaky check to make sure all is ship-shape. Satisfied that the anchor is already stowed, she pushes the basket in under the deck close by.

While the last-minute checks are being done and Bosun and Rope are busy chatting, nobody notices an unexpected passenger leap aboard until it's too late. It's Painter, the cat.

"Painter, what are you doing here? – really you don't miss a trick!"

"Rope, are you OK with Painter joining us?" asks Sheet.

Rope is too excited to worry about having too many aboard – the more the merrier, he thinks. With that, he takes command, signalling Sheet to climb aboard. She settles herself next to the cat and confirms to Rope that yes, she did have time to bake his favourite apple pies for the picnic. Seconds later, Rope pushes off to catch the tide. Sheet is proud of him as he confidently takes the tiller and steers out to the picnic spot.

As the voyage proceeds, Rope's tummy begins rumbling loudly and he begins to lose focus on helming as he sees Painter sniffing around the picnic basket. "Paws off!" he tells the cat, and Sheet nudges the basket so that it is further out of temptation.

Rope settles again and begins to demonstrate what he has learnt on the sailing course: he tries to hold the stick properly – "oops not a stick, it's a tiller." One day he'll get its name right first time, but he's happy that he is holding it properly today.

Sheet is taking sights on other passing boats and swimmers, waving and smiling and telling them all that Rope is taking her on a picnic. As well as steering, Rope is aware of the tide and he also double checks his knots. All fine, he thinks. He starts to hope that this little boat will soon be his to name, once Sheet tells Bosun how competent he has become.

Any minute now, Rope expects to see Halyard and Half-Hitch. He and Sheet have been sailing for more than twenty minutes and he remembers Halyard telling him the spot will be a short distance after the 8th red buoy. Rope begins to wonder if it is possibly the yellow buoys, not the red ones and realises he stopped counting after passing the 5th buoy. But what colour was the 5th buoy? – he is now completely confused.

Luckily for Rope, Sheet recognises the sandbanks they are just passing and expects to see Halyard and Half-Hitch waiting just around the next bend. Even the cat takes an interest and puts her head up for a look around.

Rope first hears a bark, then seconds later spots Halyard waving. First of all, Rope thinks he'll steer into earshot of Halyard, but then changes his mind and stops the boat short. He only takes the little boat as close as he dares to the banks, worrying that he will go aground if he gets too near the shallows. But now his mind is a blank – he forgets everything he learnt last week. Halyard is shouting something about throwing the anchor out early, which is not helping him solve the problem of getting ashore.

Where is the anchor? Rope panics because he can't see it, thinking that he has forgotten to bring it onboard. He looks sheepishly at Sheet who takes control, leaning down and sliding the picnic basket to one side. Underneath is a funny-shaped metal thing. Ah! – the anchor.

In his haste to show Sheet that all is fine, he leans down to reach the anchor and accidentally lets go of the helm. Suddenly the little boat is wobbling all over the place. Rope tries to steady himself and grabs hold of the mast. He remembers that he needs to throw the anchor over the side.

But within a very short time, and without Rope realising what is happening, the boat has drifted with the tide, carrying it into much deeper water than he anticipates.

Sheet leaps into action. She lets off the sheet to loosen the mainsail and slow the boat down and at the same time tries to steady the boat while Rope swings the anchor high into the air. Following instructions, Rope moves forward of the mast towards the bow and then throws the anchor out. Involved at the helm, Sheet realises too late that the anchor is airborne with no rope attached to it!

Rope hears Halyard and Sheet shout in unison "Too late – you haven't tied it on!"

Sheet kicks herself for forgetting to check earlier on whether Rope had fixed a line to the anchor. Rope watches the anchor curve into space then crash with a mighty splash into the water, all traces of it vanishing as the water closes over it.

Rope stands by the mast with a look of disbelief, annoyed with himself for thinking, just moments ago, how well things are going. He tries to cover his embarrassment and tells the others he's sure he'll find it in a jiffy.

Rope believes it will be easy to find. He thinks that all he needs do is to jump in, look down, and there will be the anchor. But he forgets that every moment the tide is taking the boat further out into deeper water, away from the place the anchor went in. He points, convinced he can see a few remaining ripples from its entry into the sea. Sheet and Halyard are not so sure, but they like his optimism.

Ready to jump in, Rope pulls off his top. Twenty minutes later, and there's no sign of it. He realises it is not as simple as he'd hoped. By this time, Sheet and Halyard have lost interest, chatting about what they'll be helping Bosun with the following day, trying to distract themselves from their hunger and the tempting smells coming from the picnic hamper.

"Hurry up! We're getting hungry," they shout to Rope.

"I think I might have it now."

Rope begins to remember something he was taught the previous week about how to locate the actual spot the anchor went in. It's a bit late, perhaps, but he recalls that if he can remember a landmark on the shore to pinpoint the place the anchor submerged, he will be able to find it.

"Hey presto – there's the 8th yellow buoy!"

Glancing at his waterproof watch, Rope realises he has already wasted over an hour. He dives down and pulls up something that feels like the anchor, but is not. He recovers an odd collection of things from the sea bottom including; a smart peaked cap, a pair of sunglasses and an old shoe that looks remarkably like one Halyard lost ages ago. Feeling a bit silly, Rope suddenly notices a shiny thing sticking up a few feet away in the shallows. Triumphantly he lifts the anchor!

Sheet remains holding the little boat afloat as she stands chatting to Halyard at the water's edge. Painter and Half-Hitch are digging holes in the sand and chasing birds.

Rope comes up with the anchor in his hand. Ignoring the untouched picnic basket, he ties the anchor firmly to a line, and the other end of the line firmly to the boat, before making any further suggestions for today.

Before he can plant the anchor in the sand further up the beach, Sheet says "Guys, we'd better head back. Bosun expressly instructed me that he wants us out of the water and packed away before the other boats that are racing today finish their race. We promised to help him and there is so much to get ready for the regatta tomorrow."

Halyard looks at his watch, ignoring Rope's haul of seabed trophies. "Yes, we have twenty minutes if we leave now. Sorry the beach picnic will have to wait for another day."

Glum faces all round. Halyard calls to Half-Hitch who waddles reluctantly across the sand, first inspecting the little boat before climbing onto the paddle-board. Painter pounces onto the little boat and looks very content as she curls up next to the picnic basket – still untouched and smelling delicious.

Rope is secretly relieved the picnic is cancelled because he can't wait to get out of his sodden clothes. He waits for Sheet to give the nod, pushes off the boat which is now on a course to the beach by the Boat-Shed.

"Ah, never mind," he says to himself.

Halyard might have felt he'd missed out on the beach picnic, but he knows his favourite pies are still in the hamper, ready to eat when they reach home. He is also looking forward to telling Bosun about Rope's fiasco with the untied anchor, and hopes to dine out on that anecdote for a while. He giggles as he paddles and this makes the board wobble.

At the water's edge, Rope and Sheet slide the trolley under the boat's hull."I'll do this," says Rope, "it's the least I can do and Halyard can help me if necessary."

"OK if you're sure," replies Sheet. "I'll lay out the picnic by the time you get back."

"Sounds like a good deal," says Rope.

Swinging the picnic basket, Sheet hurries off in the direction of the Boat-House.

Bosun, meanwhile, has seen everything through his binoculars: from Rope throwing the anchor overboard to their safe arrival back on shore. He has also noticed the untouched picnic basket under Sheet's arm. He cannot work out, though, why she has left Rope to pack away the little boat, but he's sure to find out soon. Unable to control his curiosity, he downs his tools and heads back to the Boat-House to find out why.

Rope, having eaten nothing since breakfast, is starving and his tummy is rumbling very loudly as he fastens the last of the toggles on the boat cover. At that moment, an image of his brother eating the last sausage roll flashes through his mind. Eager not to miss out on the picnic for a second time, Rope collects his gear and dashes back to the Boat-House.

Settled around the table in the comfort of the kitchen, they all watch as the hamper is finally opened. There is plenty for all, including their unexpected diner. The sandwiches go down a treat; Rope lets Halyard have the last sausage roll, Sheet gets first pick of cakes. She selects Rope's favourite, as a joke, then pushes it across to him.

"It's got your name on it."

While Rope tucks into the cake, Halyard recounts the story of the anchor flying through the air. Bosun knows that he himself has done the same thing a few times, when he was first learning to sail. He turns around, gives Rope a wink and then says to Halyard,

"That looks very much like your lost shoe, no?"

Halyard goes red and quiet at the same time, and quickly changes the subject.

"What can we help you with tomorrow, Bosun?"

Attention has switched to the things Rope found underwater, so Halyard receives no reply. They sit back, reflect on the day and Rope shows off his new pair of sunglasses, and the peak cap which is still slightly wet. With his tummy full, the anchor experience behind him, Rope feels he can congratulate himself under his breath for finding this great pair of sunglasses and the cap – and of course, in the future, he won't ever forget to check that everything's tied on properly before he sets sail!

3

Regatta day

Lots of flags raised and lowered and a shore winner

Rope wakes early – first in the Boat-House – bursting with excitement after last night's briefing and eager to share his latest idea. Tiptoeing out of his bedroom he steals into Halyard's room. His brother is still sleeping peacefully.

Rope gives Halyard a gentle nudge but there's no response. *Drastic measures* are called for, thinks Rope. He turns on the bedside light and edges towards the door, ready to make a quick exit from the room if needed.

"Morning Bro!" he says in a cheery, loud manner.

"Oh seriously, Rope," yawns Halyard. "Do you know what the

54

time is? Look, even Half-Hitch hasn't stirred yet."

Halyard turns over and pulls the covers over his head. But Rope won't give up.

"Guess what, I've got an idea of how I can thank Bosun," he says.

"You can thank him, and me, by going back to bed," replies Halyard.

"Won't you even hear me out?" pleads Rope. Halyard knows that when Rope gets something into his head, it's best to listen or else!

"Rope, you're impossible," he sighs. "OK, what is it?"

"I thought we could help Bosun by tying all the flags on!"

"I thought you said you wanted to help Bosun. Where does 'we' come into it?"

"Ah yes… well, it's just that you know the flags so well. And it's much more fun doing things with you than on my own," replies Rope. He has a way of making his ideas rather appealing, so that his brother will be unable to resist.

"OK", he concedes, stretching. "You win, since you put it like that. First you'd better be quiet and not wake the rest of the Boat-House. Off with you….while I get dressed remember to scribble a note to say where we've gone. Let them know we've gone ahead to the race start box."

Rope bounces off to dress.

Half an hour later they are at the Boat-Shed, faced with a huge pile of loose flags. Their mission is to tie-on various flags to a system of ropes, which the race organisers will use to signal the countdown for start of each race during the Regatta. The flags must be clearly visible to all sailors taking part out on the water for each race and each kind of boat, so that everyone knows exactly when their race starts.

"What were you thinking Rope? Have you any idea which flag goes up first?"

"Were you listening at the briefing?" Rope counters, throwing the question back to Halyard.

After a short pause Rope suggests they start by tying-on the one on the top of the pile first. Not totally convinced, but with no alternative idea, Halyard decides to run with Rope's idea. He picks up a bundle of flags and passes them to Rope. "You'd better start tying them on – off you go."

Meanwhile, back at the Boat-House, Sheet thought she'd heard the boys moving around earlier. What were they doing up so early? Probably one of Rope's harebrained ideas. With a busy day ahead, she decides to opt for a peaceful half hour in bed.

Plumping her pillows, she nestles back to enjoy reading a chapter of her book – a story about heading to the mountains. With a balmy summer morning outside her window, it's initially hard to imagine the cold weather and snowy setting of the story, but after a few pages Sheet is gripped. She even shivers, reading about the freezing breeze that blows into the face of the main character who skis down the piste – the snowy route leading down from the mountain top – conjuring in her mind's eye skis speeding over the clean, white snow.

By now, over at the Boat-Shed, the boys are in a pickle. Not just a few flags, but the whole lot tied on and looking a mess.

"I'm sure it's not meant to look like this," says Halyard, surveying the scene. "I've never seen the halyards so full on previous Regatta Days."

"What shall I do?" asks Rope.

"No good asking me."

Rope's face is a picture of confusion. Why is his brother's name the same as the halyard they are tying the flags to? He knows, from his sailing lessons, that a halyard is a rope that is attached vertically to a mast, allowing sails to be hoisted and lowered. Unusual to find it used as a first name, he thinks.

Halyard steps back and looks at their handy work, or not-so-handy work. Besides the fact that the flags look a total mess, none are actually flying. They hang, lifeless, on the halyards.

All the while, Rope's tummy is rumbling loudly, reminding him that he has skipped breakfast. The next rumble is so loud, it sounds like a full bath as you pull out the plug. Both boys double up with laughter, and for a moment Halyard forgets about the flags.

"I'm hungry – let's go for breakfast," suggests Rope.

"I can hear that, but we can't leave the flags now they're bent-on," replies Halyard.

His brother's foxed him again, thinks Rope, throwing in another sailing term he doesn't know.

"I thought we'd tied them on, not bent them on!"

"We did," but Halyard is too busy worrying about the flags not flying to explain to Rope what 'bent-on' means.

"Do you remember what Bosun said last night at the briefing? If the flags aren't able to fly, there's not enough wind to sail and there won't be a Regatta," he reminds Rope.

"Oh no – no breakfast *and* no Regatta. That'll be a total disaster."

"You need to start praying to the wind gods, Rope."

"OK, which way do I need to face?"

"Don't be silly, that's a myth. Once you see clouds starting to form over the land, a sea breeze should follow."

"Really? Wow!" Rope nods and pretends to understand. Yet another new word – 'sea breeze'. His head is spinning, what with 'bent-on' and 'sea breeze' – there's so much to learn about boating words. Wouldn't it be great to create a book about all this stuff, he thinks.

Wanting to show Halyard he shares his concern about wind, Rope peers up at the languid flags and shakes his head, as Halyard is doing. Ten minutes, necks now stiff, and nothing else has changed. The boys wish their sister or Bosun would hurry up and appear.

Halyard, distracted, discovers in his pocket a small handbook he's been looking for since last night.

"Look what I've found!"

"What is it?"

"It might just save our bacon!"

"Mmmm, bacon… I'm hungry."

"Shhhh, forget starvation and concentrate on the flags."

"If I have to," says Rope, peering over his brother's shoulder at the little book. "Wow, we're lucky that Bosun made this just for Regatta day. How perfect is that?"

Halyard doesn't reply, flipping the pages until he finds a section called 'Starting Sequence'. There are lots of diagrams of different flags and arrows going up and down. Rope is confused – best leave it to Halyard to fathom out.

Halyard sees that Bosun's booklet covers everything in huge detail; which flags should go up and down when, for each race in the running order of the Regatta. He glances aloft and looks at the flags that he and Rope have tied-on. Whoops, he thinks.

In the meantime, Rope's thoughts have drifted away as he watches the sailors gathering in the Boat-Park for the start of the Regatta day. They're a chatty bunch, loads of banter. He envies them, wishing he could compete in this big race, one day. Content to spectate for now, he knows that today is a good day to watch and learn.

"It's getting busy down there," he remarks, poking his brother.

"I can see that, and that's why I'm trying to sort the flags, so that, I hope, they can start on time."

"Really, are the flags that important?"

"Yes."

Halyard looks up and, thankful for small mercies, sees that the flags are beginning to flutter slightly.

Neither of the boys notice Sheet quietly approaching, secretly listening to their every word as they try and sort out the flags.

"If you untie those flags, I'll pop them on in the right order this time," she hears Halyard say.

"'This time', what do you mean 'this time'?" she asks.

Before they can answer, Sheet clocks the mess, and switches immediately to helpful mode. "What do we have here – can I help? Rope, off you go and find a box to put the flags in. I'll see if I can find the little book that shows us when to pull them up and went pull them down. I know Bosun had it somewhere."

"Sheet – it's OK, I've just found it. It's been in my pocket the whole time – I just forgot, maybe 'cos I was woken up so early," says Halyard, eyeing Rope.

"Hmmm, does that mean we have to undo them all and start again?"

A silence descends. Sheet peers over Halyard's shoulder at the little book.

"I'm afraid so," she says.

By now Halyard and Rope have been up two hours, no breakfast, and hunger has got the better of them. They struggle to concentrate.

"Sorry about breakfast, Halyard," says Rope.

"Never mind – your intentions were good, even it was a bit silly."

An encouraging voice behind them tells them there are only two more flags to go and all will be done.

Still fixated on food, Rope shouts "Halyard, can you smell egg muffins? I'm sure I can't be imagining it."

"Yes, and bacon too."

Their mouths water. Just one flag left to tie-on…

"For your sake, Rope, let's hope he doesn't arrive before we finish."

"Who arrives?" a deep voice booms. They turn, and behold! Bosun holds a tray piled high with egg and bacon muffins and some cups of chilled squash.

"I thought you might need some breakfast, having left so early," he says. Their faces light up as Bosun hands them the tray.

"You're a star, yes please!!"

With flags sorted and stomachs now full, they reflect on how Bosun operates; always thoughtful and thinking of others and today, being a busy Regatta day, is no exception.

With order restored, Sheet can complete her final briefing to her brothers about how to operate the flag system. She has their full attention.

"Finally, the flags and horns happen at the same time – have you got it? – and remember, Bosun will give us a countdown so please listen out for this. It's very important."

Excited and nervous in equal measure, they both try to reassure her by smiling. Halyard is first to break the silence. "We'll keep our ears pricked, I promise."

"I'll only pull the flags up and down just as you tell me," adds Rope.

"Wonderful," says Sheet.

Rope checks his watch and sees it's only fifteen minutes to the start. He tries to calm the butterflies in his tummy by looking over again at the Boat-Park. Its empty... where have they all gone, he wonders?

From the corner of his eye he sees a hive of activity on the shore, with every type, or class, of dinghy imaginable down on the water. It's a magnificent sight. He watches them all, sailing in different directions, marvelling at how they can weave around and miss each other in such a confined space. Among the melee, he can see groups, or fleets, of each class of boat and within each fleet, all boats carry the same 'class flag' to help identify them.

He's found out from Halyard that all the boats appear to be trying to stay on one side of an imaginary, invisible start line. They all seem to be concentrating on their own stuff, nobody listening.

Halyard has also heard that the boat with no. 12 on the sail is tipped as a winner, and he's keen to see where the boat is positioned for the start.

With their attention elsewhere, the minutes fly by. Bosun alerts them to the final minute and to raising the first flag. The boys give him a nervous thumbs-up. Sheet looks happy and ticks another action off the list on her running order.

"Here goes, are you ready?" A few seconds later they hear a loud, clear voice. "Ten, nine, eight, seven, six, *five*, four, three"… Rope tightens the halyard, ready to pull up the first flag. "Two, one and UP!" He pulls harder, hoisting the flag till it flies at the top of the halyard. He gives a contented sigh and ties it off firmly. Sheet gives him a reassuring wink as he secures the end of the halyard into a special clip, called a cleat, that stops it slipping down again.

And while the busy flag raising sequence goes on around him, Rope sees that Bosun still has time for his normal banter. Bosun's so confident, he thinks, hoping that one day he'll grow up to have those qualities himself – confidence and thoughtfulness. Better start practicing…

Between hoisting the different flags, Rope tries to recall the time Bosun showed him how to tie his first knot. But he has to stop abruptly, and would have missed the next countdown, if Halyard hadn't kicked him. He just catches "Four, three, two, one and class flag down."

"That was a close shave," he says, looking over at Halyard who is busy sorting out the next flag he needs to pull down.

By now, most of the fleets are underway. Rope has one last flag to pull down and his duties are finished. Throughout the sequence he's heard his heart beating louder than ever before. At one point he thought it might burst. Excitement overwhelms him and he can't stop himself dissolving into uncontrolled laughter as the flag comes down.

"Shhhhhh," Halyard reproves him. "Can't you see I've got to concentrate – I've still got two flags left."

"Guys settle down!" Sheet's tone says it all. "Rope, could you be quiet a little longer so that Bosun can hear me calling out the sail numbers as they pass this mark?"

Chastened, Rope sits quietly trying to make sense of what he sees and hears, and finds confusion washing over him again. "One minute they're going round a 'buoy', now they're passing a 'mark'. Which is it?" He senses that the others are too busy to register what he just said, let alone explain it to him. "Honestly

I wish someone would invent a book on boating to make it easier to grasp this new sailing language – it's starting to do my head in."

"What's that you say?" asks Halyard.

"Nothing, just a thought."

Rope soon notices lots of chatter from the packed patio below the race start box. It sounds like a heated debate and appears to be about the start of the last race. One lady, in particular, is very vocal and Rope can tell she's keen to get her point across.

"If it was me, I would have started right in the middle of the line, not at the other end, that won't pay." Another chirps up "No, they won't have clear wind starting there."

He wanders away, wondering about the last comment and heads over to Halyard who has now finished his flag duty too.

"Halyard…?"

"Yes?"

"Does wind come in different colours?"

"What'ya on about now, Rope?"

"I just heard them talking on the patio."

"Who's they?"

"Spectators below, of course."

"Ooh them," says Halyard in a knowledgeable tone, but

conscious of only just having 'got' the concept of an imaginary start line himself.

"Have I missed something? Is there such a thing as wind having colours?"

"No, not actual colours. Let me explain. It's going to be easier to show you about wind using some props. Do you have any sweets in your pockets?"

Rope pulls some pebbles from his pocket.

"They'll do – hand them over and I'll show you what they mean about clear wind."

Rope watches Halyard lay the pebbles on the deck one by one. "Imagine two pebbles are boats, this one is wind."

"OK – are they all the same colour?"

"Forget colour for the moment."

"OK, excellent. Wind is clear." Rope flies high with this question cleared. "I'm going back to eavesdrop on that bunch again. I might learn something else from them."

Halyard walks off, shaking his head in disbelief, but glad of a few minutes breathing space to see how sailboat No. 12 is doing in the race.

Rope looks for sailboat No. 4, chosen purely as his lucky number.

The patio has emptied out in the meantime, with all spectators reconvened down by the shore. Rope thinks he can see the vocal lady from earlier, leading the group. He hears cheering and fragments of encouragement called to the sailors. "Keep it up! Remember to head away from the shore on the next leg!" He can see the lady gesticulating at the other group, then pointing to the lead boat.

"Wow, when I race I'm always going to start in the middle," thinks Rope out loud.

"Are you sure, Rope?" Halyard's voice comes from behind.

"Definitely."

Rope senses he could be on to something, especially as he is sure they all know their stuff. He likes the idea that he too could win a race from the patio. He expands on the idea. Winning a race without the hassle of getting his feet wet is ideal. Yes, it'll be a far more sensible place to race from than on the water; all the fun, no rigging up the boat, no getting wet. Rope congratulates himself for eavesdropping and discovering this concept of 'patio racing'.

Dismissing it as a ridiculous idea, Halyard walks away.

A little while later, Rope heads back to the start box to see if he's needed. Halyard is already there, tidying away the flags.

"Anything I can do, Bosun?" asks Rope.

"Go and collect the flags from Halyard and bring them to me, please. Then I'll show you where I'd like them stored."

Seconds later, Rope's back with the flags. Bosun shows Rope how the fold the flags and where to place them in their individual pigeon holes. The look of concentration on Rope's face is priceless as he carries out the instructions and Bosun has to look away to keep his own face straight.

Halyard brings another pile of flags. Between them they fold and stow the flags, checking that all are in their right places, ready for next time. It's a piece of real teamwork.

"At least this'll stop you listening to those silly spectators," remarks Halyard. "They're not out there on the water like the real sailors, are they? Honestly, whatever next?"

With all flags now put away and the end of the race imminent, the brothers leave the race start box to give Bosun and Sheet space to attend to the finishing details. After feeding their pets, Rope plans to build sandcastles and Halyard to fish just off the shoreside.

"Make sure Half-Hitch's lifejacket is fastened properly," Bosun calls to Rope. "See you both at the prize-giving tea. Remember, it starts a three o'clock sharp and look out for the team table where we've reserved seats for you."

Rope fantasises about piles of cakes and scones. "Three it is!"

With the tea plans firmly in place, the brothers link arms and run off to feed their pets, singing as they run.

After the animals have been fed and adorned in lifejackets, they all head to the beach. Half-Hitch splashes in the water to cool down, wagging his backside. Painter the cat is stationed near the end of the rod, hoping the fishing line will start to to twitch.

With his huge sandcastle half built, Rope turns to see Halyard struggling to pull in his fishing line. Rope drops his bucket, eager to see the size of the fish that Halyard has hooked. "Ooh, a big one!"

"It's pulling alright," agrees Halyard, but then the line suddenly slackens. Painter's gaze shifts to the horizon, hoping for another fish.

Thus engaged, neither of the boys notice that the boats are all back ashore. A loudspeaker announcement floats over to their part of the beach.

Seconds later, Bosun appears. "Time for tea, boys. Sheet's doing her final checks and when she's handed out the prizes, she'll join us for a swim."

"Handing out prizes, a swim... how cool is that?" murmurs Rope. "You know in films they normally get a bunch of flowers at the end of the ceremony... will Sheet get one?"

"Maybe" says Bosun, trying to keep it a surprise. "Come on guys, before everyone else eats all the cakes!"

"Can we bring the pets?"

"Yes, but put Half-Hitch on a lead – we know what he gets up to when he's too excited."

Rope is taken aback by the size of the crowd gathered for the prize-giving tea. The queue for the cake table is already long. "Look Halyard, at those flapjacks by the chocolate brownies!"

His mouth begins to water and suddenly he's being steered to the front of the queue by Bosun to have first dibs of the cakes, and all because he helped with the flags. Worth getting up early, after all, he thinks.

Another thing he's observed about today's Regatta is that everyone likes to be in the same place at the same time. First the crowd in the Boat-Park this morning, then the imaginary start line where everyone lines up together, and now here again at the cake table. He begins to wonder if there might be a better way to do this!

"A healthy appetite after my own heart, Rope," says a passing voice, as he sees plate after plate piled high with scones and cakes.

During prize-giving, Rope looks round for the vocal lady from the patio. He's still convinced she's going to win a prize. A seat is reserved for him in the front row, giving him a prime spot from which to watch the proceedings.

A hush descends on the crowd as Bosun stands. Opening the ceremony, he thanks everyone for coming and invites Sheet to present the prizes. All helpers are asked to stand and the crowd claps loudly. Halyard and Rope are last to be thanked, blushing as they stand to take their applause. Sheet is truly proud of her brothers and their lovely smiles.

Rope can't see the vocal patio sailor anywhere among the winners. "Strange," he says "I was sure she'd win something," but remembering his brother's opinion of patio sailing, he doesn't expand on the comment.

Despite this, he finds the whole atmosphere magical – the applause, the happiness of the winners as they collect their awards. He pledges that one day, he'll be a top dinghy sailor himself and not a patio sailor, after all.

The second the prize-giving is over, the crowd disperses. "Time for a swim!" chirps Rope.

Ten minutes later they are all down at the beach when Bosun appears, running towards them with his arms full of flippers and goggles. "Wait for me! I thought these would be fun to swim in!" he shouts. "It'll give you an idea of how fast Sammy can swim."

Rope is delighted. For once, he'll be able to keep up with his pet. "Bosun – first tea, now this. Such a cool day! Thank you, the best summer holiday I've ever had."

"OK. Let's stay in the shallows to begin with. Find our feet first."

Halyard helps Rope into his flippers and Sheet helps the boys demist their goggles.

"On the count of three – let's all run together!"

Arms linked, ready, *steady,* **go!!** Roars of laughter as they try to run in the flippers, falling akimbo as they go. Swimming turns to hunt-the-flipper and catch-the-goggle. Then one last swim to round off the afternoon and they are all competitive again.

"What's a swim off?"

With no further explanation, Sheet blows her whistle. "Get in line, ready, steady, let's go!"

"Ready for what? – tell us more!"

Sheet dives in. Seconds later all are hot on her heels. They catch her as she rounds a moored dinghy, now neck-and-neck till Bosun takes the lead by a whisker. Then a sprint to the shore that looks to be the finish, everyone throwing everything they've got to catch him up. Hitting the beach, they are caked in sand and spluttering with delight. All shout "I won!" With nobody to judge who came first, Sheet calls a dead heat.

Meanwhile, participating from the beach, Half-Hitch races up and down the water's edge, barking loudly. Setting an altogether more dignified tone, Painter stretches out and basks in the sun.

"8 o'clock," says Sheet, checking her watch and gathering her things together. "Better head back now."

"Thanks Bosun, another great day pulling the flags up and down," chorus the boys.

"And yes, remind me to stay in bed next time Rope comes up with a silly idea," says Halyard.

Rope is already half way home, to be first in the bathroom.

Later, all settle down for a night cap before bed. Rope is first to depart for bed, with a great big smile as he thanks them all again "Night all." Climbing the stairs he sings that great retro classic 'We're all going on a summer holiday.' Ten minutes later he fast asleep, dreaming about another Regatta day.

4

The alternative regatta – without flags

After a blissful night's sleep, Rope wakes up full of beans, a new dream fresh in his mind. Hearing Sheet's and Halyard's voices already downstairs, he is keen to share his dream *right now!*

Rope has noticed in the last few weeks – since he started sailing in fact – that he's now able to dress without a fuss and without delay and that he's always in a happy mood. Today is no exception and he bounces down the stairs, two at a time.

"You're looking very pleased with yourself," remarks Sheet.

Strange as it may seem, the Boat-House always senses when

Rope has a new idea.

"Why the hurry?" pipes up Halyard "Come on, spill the beans."

"Oh, is it that obvious?" asks Rope, while he tries to remember the new dream in full. He pauses for a few seconds, before saying with a hint of mystery "Yes, as far as I am concerned today's the day there aren't any flags."

"What?"

But Rope makes no further comment and with his dream engaging his full attention, loses himself in his own thoughts. Oblivious to his surroundings, he fails to look what he's doing as he tries to squeeze into his seat next to his brother. He accidentally nudges Halyard who is holding the milk jug and milk spills far and wide across the breakfast table.

"Rope – look what you made me do!"

By now, milk is dribbling down the leg of the table, onto the floor and onto the cat, Painter, who is an innocent bystander beneath. It was clear that Painter hadn't bargained for this either. Only moments before she had been sitting peacefully under the table, waiting for some titbit to fall on the floor – some bacon perhaps – but not a torrent of milk *to lick*.

To avoid the drips, she leaps to the safety of Sheet's lap.

"Get off – you're covered in milk!" Sheet shoos the cat off her lap. *Yet again*, within moments of Rope's appearance on the scene, *there seems to be chaos.*

Before Sheet has time to do anything, Rope grabs Painter, picks up a dish cloth, first wiping the cat's paws before setting her safely down out of harm's reach, back on the window cill. Finally he mops up the milk under the table too.

Sheet is impressed by his quick actions and proud to see her little brother quickly growing up in front of her very eyes.

Now, with calm restored to the kitchen, they take their places, Rope once again between Sheet and Halyard. However, this time he takes more care as he sits down. Sheet is busy concentrating on filling her cereal bowl, whilst Halyard gazes out of the window, trying to see why Painter seems transfixed by something she has seen outside.

Rope, meanwhile, is still keen to share his dream and hasn't stopped to think that after such an action-packed day yesterday, his brother and sister might just fancy a bit of peace and quiet at breakfast this morning.

No – Rope has other ideas. He launches straight in. "Fancy joining me on my non-flags day?" And without drawing breath, he's off, reminding them of the shenanigans of pulling all the flags up and down during yesterday's racing. "What were we thinking, Halyard, getting up so early – and missing breakfast!? What topped it off for me, was having to re-tie all the flags again and all before we even started the real flag sequence..."

Halyard quickly butts in, "Yes but once I found the book..."

"Hold on," Rope interrupts before his brother can finish "if it wasn't for Sheet's calmness, or that Bosun came to our rescue with those yummy bacon butties, I think we might have possibly lost the plot. Talking of Bosun, has anyone seen him?"

"Yes, he said he'll be back in an hour," Sheet looks down at her watch, "we can expect him back any second – with Half-Hitch."

"Great – I'd like him to be here when I share my news," says Rope.

"I hope after yesterday, you've thought today's idea through more carefully?"

Rope ignores Halyard's comment and continues to labour the point about all the flag pulling yesterday morning. "Do you know, I will need twelve months to practise if I'm going to get it right next year."

"Why – are you thinking of helping next year?"

"No silly, I'm going to sail in the regatta next year. No flag pulling for me, it's far too confusing."

"Good on you – a great idea. Is this the news you were going to tell us, before you spilt the milk?"

Rope blushes before answering, realising that he has gone way off track for getting to the point about the no-flag day. He shakes his head, collecting his thoughts.

"No – I'm proposing an 'alternative regatta day' and why

couldn't we have it today, of all days, as the weather is perfect?"

Neither Sheet nor Halyard could disagree with him on that.

Intrigued, Halyard looks up from his plate. "What are you thinking?"

"First, there'd be no flags to start with."

"OK, got that. What else?"

Rope has been hoping that, by now, Bosun would have arrived and could have helped him flesh out the idea, but unfortunately there's no sign of him. He's about to forge ahead with the plans, when, as if by magic, Bosun arrives as if from nowhere.

"Your ears must have been burning!"

"Why?"

"Nothing."

Instead of coming straight in, Bosun remains at the back door.

"I need your help guys. Can one of you come and sort out Half-Hitch? He's jumped in the mud and he's caked from head to toe. He smells too – I don't want him anywhere inside this Boat-House in this state."

"He's your dog. Halyard. Remember, I have Sammy."

Halyard ignores Rope's silly remark.

"Can I leave you to sort him – sorry, I have to dash? He's tied up and quite happy, eating, so no hurry. Finish your breakfast first."

"It's ok, we haven't really started."

"It'd be easier if the two of you clean him down together. As I said, must dash," and in a flash, Bosun is gone.

Outside the back door is a trail of mess.

Sheet feels a pang of guilt because it was her suggestion that Half-Hitch should go fishing instead of Painter. She thinks to herself that the least she can do is to offer them a cooked breakfast.

"Guys, if you sort out Half-Hitch, I'll knock up some bacon butties and we can finish talking about the 'alternative without flag day' when you two are done," she says.

The prospect of bacon *two days in a row* sees the boys legging it out the door, armed with buckets and sponges, in record time. "Great idea!" they reply in unison.

As soon as they see Half-Hitch, they understand why Bosun was reluctant to let him indoors.

"Good job Bosun tied him up."

"If you clean the wall and back door, I'll get the worst off the dog," suggests Rope.

"Good thinking," replies his brother who is tall enough to reach the high mud splats at the top of the wall. They set to work.

If it weren't for Half-Hitch's signature bottom-wag, he would be virtually unrecognisable, coated all over in glutinous black mud. With his paws nearly double their normal size, thanks to the mud slicks between his toes, he looks almost web-footed – certainly nothing like an English Bulldog.

Rope tackles the clean-up in two phases; first by hosing mud off Half-Hitch's paws and then setting to work with a sponge.

Anyone who's ever been faced with the same challenge knows it's a really filthy job. Each time Rope hoses the dog down, Half-Hitch responds with another backside-wag that sprays even more muck onto the wall of the Boat-House as well as all over Rope.

After yet another splat of mud hits the wall that he has just painstakingly cleaned, Halyard drops his sponge into the bucket with disgust.

"I give up – I'm not winning here! If you carry on hosing him down, you should have got the worst off him by the time I get back. I'm off to find a jet-washer – it's got to be quicker than using a sponge."

"OK, and you might just have to jet-wash me too," adds Rope.

His brother laughs, and heads off to the Boat-Shed in search of a jet-washer.

Ten minutes later, thanks to a lot of elbow grease, Half-Hitch is transformed back into an English Bulldog. Halyard is back with the jet-washer and a long power lead.

"Ah, he's looking better already."

"Yes – shame about the wall."

"No worries, I'll have that sorted in no time with this contraption," and he uncoils the lead and plugs in.

Aromas of savoury bacon begin to drift from the interior of the Boat-House. It is a clever knack of Sheet's that she has learnt over the years – how to press the right buttons to hurry her brothers up.

"Do hurry! Something smells awfully good," urges Rope.

To finish the job more quickly, Halyard asks Rope to find a towel for the dog and a clean lead as well.

Within minutes, back in the Boat-House, things are in order. Painter sits contentedly on the windowsill, peering out, her eyes fixed on the birds.

A now-pristine Half-Hitch takes his normal place under the table, while the three siblings munch on much-appreciated bacon sandwiches in companionable silence.

Rope savours his last mouthful, his train of thought momentarily derailed by the spilt milk and muddy dog episodes that have claimed the morning so far. It's only Sheet's nudge and a prompt to tell them more about his dream, that switches Rope back onto his new non-flag theme.

"Ah yes, thanks for reminding me, I'd almost forgotten. The idea that came from my dream seemed so simple at the time, and so much less confusing than yesterday. I just have to tell you about it – and the best thing is that we're all able to take part in it. How does that sound?"

"Confusing… try me again," replies Halyard who is listening eagerly.

Rope tries to sound enthusiastic, although he knows he is repeating himself for the umpteenth time. "Yes, after yesterday, the perfect thing about today's regatta is there's no need for any flags."

"Did you say we can all join in?" chirps Sheet.

"Yes, and with no flags. How perfect is that?"

Quiet descends as they set to, mulling over Rope's harebrained idea. Could it possibly work?

Each ticking second of silence unnerves Rope so that his first impulse is to abandon the whole thing. He has convinced himself that they don't get his new idea. He's almost thinking, oh well, it was a stupid dream anyway.

And then Sheet says "I rather like the idea of an alternative regatta day – I think it has a great ring to it."

Halyard smiles. "I like the novelty of the no flags idea too."

Rope is taken off-guard for a second. "Are you two serious?"

"Yes."

"Let's hurry and clear the table, then we can get going."

"Ok Rope, go and clean your teeth first and get ready for sailing. We'll clear up here."

"Thanks," says Rope, heading upstairs, humming and feeling rather pleased with himself.

Once in the bathroom, and thankful for these few moments alone, he is wondering what he should include in this 'alternative regatta day'. Without Bosun to help him fill in the gaps in the idea, he is on his own. He peers into the mirror, smiling at his reflection, and says "you and your dream – whatever next?"

Downstairs, Halyard and Sheet are pooling their ideas about the alternative regatta. Sheet has an inkling that Rope's ideas were sketchy at best, but she is happy to go along with his idea anyway.

Rope, now fully dressed for boating, passes them on the stairs.

"We've stacked the dishwasher. Would you mind drying up the last things that are left on the side?" Sheet asks him.

"For sure!" he replies, prepared to do anything she asks because he is so excited by what he hopes is the next step to becoming a competent sailor. Alone again with the dishes, he racks his brains to extract more details of the dream, putting the last few plates away. "If only I could remember…"

Behind him the back door clicks open.

"Ah Rope, great to see that Half-Hitch is sorted and back in his normal place," says Bosun.

"Yes, but he seems quieter than usual."

"Give him a little while and he'll be back to normal."

"I'm beginning to miss his normal behaviour."

"Changing the subject, Rope, I can see you're planning something – I can see in your eyes. Why not fill me in quickly?"

"Oh yes! We're going to have an 'alternative flag day'." In his hurry, the words came out in the wrong order.

"Halyard and Sheet are upstairs getting ready – they absolutely love the idea."

"Really?"

"There is a minor matter – I still have no idea how to run it!"

"You'll be fine. Just remember the secret in all planning – keep it simple, then I'm sure it will all be fine."

Rope smiles and finishes the dishes.

Even though Bosun is intrigued, he has jobs to finish before he's more involved. "OK, I'll come down to the beach as soon as I'm done. It sounds like a lot of fun! By the way, remember to tell the others not to leave before I've checked the conditions. If all goes well, I'll be there pretty soon."

As he's about the shut the back door behind him, Bosun leans back into the room and says "I'll be happy to help if you like?"

"Like? *Love it!* – yes please."

The kitchen is silent once more, and this time Rope remembers every bit of detail from his dream. He laughs to himself – how strangely things work out. So far today, nothing has gone to plan. "Oh dear, what was I thinking?" he murmurs aloud.

Back upstairs, Sheet is hunting for her whistle which she thinks will come in handy. Halyard is halfway out the bedroom door when he remembers he's forgotten the chart of the harbour and doubles back to pick it up.

Rope turns round when he hears their voices, excited and rackety on the stairs. "Was that Bosun's voice I heard?"

"Yes," says Rope, buoyed up with his new-found confidence, "and the great news is, he's *promised to help* too."

"Wonderful!"

"Just a second, you two, what's the plan?"

"We can sort out the finer points as we get rigged-up."

"Rope, sometimes you are impossible, but I am sure somehow, between us, we'll get it sorted."

Rope is relieved to hear Sheet say that, knowing full well he has been winging it up to now. He follows the others out of the back door.

"Haven't you forgotten someone Halyard?"

"Have I?" murmurs Halyard as he picks up his paddle. And there, waiting patiently under the table to be called, is Half-Hitch. "How unlike his normal character to act so sheepishly."

"P'rhaps he still thinks he's in the dog house."

"And rightly so. Come on Half-Hitch – time for boating." Within a split second, the dog is bouncing around, wagging and back to his usual excitable self.

"Watch out!! He's going to knock something over – let's hurry."

After three weeks at the Boat-House, the three of them have the exit manoeuvres off to a tee. Sheet holds the door; Rope clears the path ahead and picks up Halyard's paddle, leaving his brother to buckle Half-Hitch into his lifejacket. It's a seamless team effort.

They are just a few metres from the Boat-Park when Sheet suddenly asks "Where's Painter?"

"She sneaked out with Bosun while you were upstairs."

"That's great – one fewer to worry about," she thinks.

Still in seamless team mode, they first untie Sheet's boat cover as they listen to Rope's very scratchy plans. Luckily for Rope, his brother and sister have their own ideas about the best way to approach the start of the new race. Rope is delighted that he shared his dream after all.

"Will this be useful?" asks Sheet, producing her whistle from her pocket.

"For sure, we can use it for the start."

Sheet beams her widest smile, happy she brought it along.

But suddenly the atmosphere changes as Rope announces that he's going to check on Sammy's whereabouts.

"Why?" say both his siblings at the same time.

"In my dream, Sammy leads us round the harbour."

"You can't be serious!"

"Why not? Remember he lives in it and knows the harbour better than any of us."

At this point, Halyard hides his harbour chart in the sail bag for safe keeping. He and Sheet are speechless, but in a bid to humour Rope, they just roll their eyes in disbelief.

"OK, we're off to round up Painter – I think she's in the Boat-Shed with Bosun," says Sheet, changing the subject.

"OK, I'll finish off rigging your boat," says Rope while Sheet hurries off behind Halyard.

Confident that his plan is now all set to go, Rope turns his attention to the last few adjustments to 'Come Alongside', all the while scanning the harbour for Sammy. He secretly wishes Bosun would appear again before his siblings return, so that he can run his idea past him first.

Having spotted his pet, Rope feels sure that using Sammy to guide the three of them around the nooks and crannies of the harbour will certainly inject some fun into the day – and he begins to believe that his plan cannot go wrong.

Meanwhile, Sheet decides to return to the Boat-House before she looks for Painter. She makes a beeline for the rather smelly fridge that Bosun uses to keep his daily catches, because she's had an idea that could just save Rope's plan – fish! A combination of fish and Painter's watchful nature, she hopes, might mean that Rope's silly idea of following Sammy round the harbour could just work… If she can keep Sammy in sight for a couple of hours, all be will fine.

Sheet puts all of Bosun's morning catch into a bucket and heads for the backdoor. On her way she spies Bosun's captain cap dangling on the coat stand. That could be a really fitting hat for Rope for the day, given that he is in charge, but she can't suggest it to her brother until she has asked Bosun first.

While Sheet's in the Boat-House, Halyard is on the lookout for Painter over at the Boat-Shed. There he finds the cat and

Bosun, over by the tool cupboard.

"Bosun, glad I caught you."

"What is it?"

"You remember yesterday that some of the spectators looked rather dapper – do you think I should dress up too?"

Bosun is not sure why Halyard wants to make a big thing of the day by dressing up, but smiles and replies "Yes, if you like. That would be a lovely idea. What I've heard so far is that Rope is organising something rather special for today, based on a dream he had last night."

"Yes, you're right. Personally I think it's a bit silly, but I can't resist his enthusiasm. Have you heard the latest?" asks Halyard.

"No."

"He plans to involve Sammy as our guide around the harbour!"

"Sounds interesting... I'm sure it'll be fun! When you go, will you please take Painter?"

"Almost forgot her – yes, that's why I popped in anyway," murmurs Halyard as Painter starts purring.

"Perfect. Could you tell the others I'm on my way once I've finished this? I did promise to help and it sounds like you might need some extra assistance if Rope's dream idea is going to work."

"That's probably an understatement but I always like Rope's harebrained schemes. It'll be fun, if nothing else."

With that, Halyard heads out in the wrong direction and arrives at the Boat-House with the cat under his arm. On the back porch he bumps into Sheet carrying a stinky bucket of fish. He looks at her for a second, but feeling sure she has her reasons for doing so, decides not to ask.

As the bucket wafts past, Painter leaps from Halyards' arms and glues herself to Sheet's side. Sheet in turn picks her up to be sure she can't steal any of the fish.

Conditions are ideal for sailing and she hopes that Rope will have prepared 'Come Alongside' properly for the day's adventures. On arrival she's delighted to see that he has rigged the dinghy for sailing. Looking round to thank him, she spots Rope down at the shoreline, scanning the harbour.

Whilst he is preoccupied, Sheet takes a few moments to attach – in secret – a small sack of fish to the bottom of the rudderstock of Rope's little boat. That done, she beckons him over.

"Rope, what are you looking for?"

"Sammy, of course."

"Have you seen him?"

"Yes, his head just popped up over there," replies Rope, pointing.

"Oh wow, that's great news!"

"He must be waiting to lead us around the harbour!"

Less convinced, Sheet decides to change the subject.

"Thanks for rigging my boat – it's perfect. Next time I see Bosun, I'll tell him you rigged my dinghy."

"That'd be great, if you would."

Throughout the conversation, Painter has been struggling in Sheet's arms, desperate to find a way to get to the fish in the bucket – she has no time for studying birds in the sky today. Sheet puts the cat gently down, so she can continue her conversation with Rope without getting scratched.

With Sheet's eyes distracted for a fraction of a second, Painter seizes her chance. In the blink of an eye, her nose is straight in the bucket, she grabs a tail and swallows a fish whole. Rope sees her, and, closest to the bucket he bends down to grab her. With her appetite sated, the cat doesn't resist and licks her paws contentedly.

"Those aren't for you," Rope tells the cat as he picks her up, wondering at the same instant, who the fish *are* for. He decides not to ask Sheet for the moment, but he does have an inkling of his own.

"Rope, can you watch Painter? I've a few things to sort out," asks Sheet.

"Sure."

Painter wriggles free of Rope's grasp and then, to his surprise, jumps willingly into his little boat without needing any encouragement to embark. Odd, he thinks, because the cat always prefers to sail with Sheet. Oh well, the company will nice on his first race. "Wow – my first race," he says to the cat who is purring loudly.

The race today, thinks Rope to himself, presents an excellent opportunity to build his confidence – helming the boat and following Sammy as well. Yes, he will be another step closer to naming his own boat! How cool is that? At the same time, oblivious to the secret sack and its contents, Rope has no idea why Painter is really so happy to be on board with him.

Back at the Boat-House, Halyard is having second thoughts about dressing up for the race, but he decides to press on and find his blazer anyway. He rummages through the entire wardrobe before finding it on the last hanger at the back.

Parading in front of the mirror, he is surprised to find that it fits, after a fashion. He's grown a lot in the preceding year, so it's a little short in the arms, but otherwise fine for one more outing. Sporting the bold striped blazer, he heads back to the beach to join the others, whistling and skipping. He's feeling confident, thanks to all the training he's had from Bosun recently. He thinks it's going to be an easy win for him. But as he catches sight of Half-Hitch in his lifejacket, waiting patiently on the back of his paddle-board, he feels a flicker of doubt… he must offload the dog if he wants to win, otherwise the animal's extra weight will really slow him down.

Halyard looks across at Rope, wondering if he's missed his chance there as Painter has already bagged a place on board his younger brother's boat. Rope is waiting at the water's edge, keen to get going, but had earlier promised Bosun that they wouldn't set off without his say-so. So Halyard heads over to ask Sheet instead.

While all this is going on, Bosun has lost track of time, and is then distracted by the sight of Halyard sporting his old blazer.

Instantly curious, he downs tools and strides off to find out what the three children are up to.

Seeing Bosun exit the Boat-Shed, Halyard says to Rope, "Look, Bosun's on his way! I can see him." Halyard darts over to Rope to see if he needs any help.

"Yes please," replies Rope. "By the way, love your blazer."

"Thanks. I thought your Alternative Regatta Day warranted dressing up for," rejoins Halyard.

Sheet looks over at them and calls to Rope, "That reminds me, I might have something for you – let me check first with Bosun."

Enjoying the mystery of Sheet's suggestion, and the sartorial effort Halyard has gone to with the blazer, Rope thinks he too, might like to dress up for the day.

Attending to some last minute checks on 'Come Alongside', Sheet glances up to see Sammy – easily recognisable with his white spot on his nose – splashing around in the shallows, apparently focusing all attention on Rope. She smiles to herself. "Very interesting," she thinks.

Her plan seems to be working! Sammy must have picked up the scent from the secret sack. Sheet is beginning to warm to the idea that Sammy might just play a part in the race on this Alternative Regatta day after all.

"You three are keen!" says Bosun, appearing at the shoreline. "What's all the rush about? By the way, you look great in the blazer."

Halyard blushes.

"Now. what are you up to? You mentioned something about an 'alternative something' but I was preoccupied at the time.

Everyone talks at once.

"It's our Alternative Regatta Day – it's Rope's idea," pipes up Halyard.

"Yes, with no flags," chips in Rope whose boat is now floating in the water. "Wonderful idea!"

"I bought a whistle," chimes in Sheet, blowing it loudly.

Bosun laughs, somewhat surprised that Sheet is so taken with Rope's harebrained idea. And he really likes their enthusiasm. He immediately offers to blow the whistle.

"No time like the present – let's get started!"

In his excitement, Rope expands his idea. "Bosun, as Sammy knows the harbour really well, he will lead us around the course. It's going to be loads of fun!"

Smiling from ear to ear, Rope admits that, even though he only had a scratch plan an hour earlier, it's all coming together with help from his best buddies, Sheet and Halyard. He stands in the water, holding his boat and ready for the off.

"How long is your regatta race going to be?" asks Bosun.

"We'll sail as long as Sammy leads us," replies Rope.

Hearing this, Bosun's tone changes somewhat. "Ah… we might have a flaw there." To make matters worse, he then enquires about who is making the regatta tea.

"Oh no – I haven't thought of that," wails Rope.

"You always have tea on regatta day – it's tradition," Bosun reminds them.

A few silent seconds tick by before he says "OK, perhaps Julia my cleaner can knock up some sandwiches. I saw some ice cream in the freezer too – leave it to me."

Relief and smiles all round.

Bosun accepts the challenge, knowing he will be able to make the tea arrangements by the time the race ends, and that he won't need to be too involved in it himself.

"Leave it to me – I'll text Julia once I get you started."

A chorus of thanks from the children before Rope, impatient to get going, says "Does that mean we can go now?"

"How about we give Rope a five minute start?" suggests Sheet.

Halyard doesn't reply. He's busy thinking of his ambition to win. If Rope has a five minute start, it'll be impossible to catch him up with Half-Hitch is onboard, weighing them down. He HAS to come up with a plan – and quick!

In the meantime, Rope is distracted by Painter's weird behaviour. She's sitting at the stern and she's never done that on previous outings. It'll make it more difficult to helm with her there. He almost misses Sheet's offer of a headstart. "Did you say I can go first?"

"Yes, that's the plan."

"Wonderful! Can I go now?"

"Hold your horses!"

Halyard seizes his opportunity. "Sheet, it might startle Sammy to see Half-Hitch on the paddle board. Maybe he should ride with Rope and Painter, and it might help settle Painter too?"

"Good idea – if Rope agrees," she replies.

Rope is all for jumping into his boat and heading away. "How long have we got to the off?"

"Wait, Rope. Can you take Half-Hitch too?"

"Sure, the more the merrier!"

At first, this is music to Halyard's ears. He can tell Rope is delighted to help. Rope calls the dog who bounces off the paddle-board, wagging his tail, and stops at Rope's feet. The boy picks him up and puts him aboard with Painter. Half-Hitch settles by the mast and Rope is, once again, ready for the start.

But Halyard is now having second thoughts about hoodwinking his brother into taking Half-Hitch. He's feeling guilty about having an ulterior motive in the first place, quite apart from the weight advantage he has managed to negotiate himself, and he knows Rope's hands will be full with Painter on board anyway. What's got into the cat today, he wonders?

Rope hasn't noticed the brief conversation between Sheet and Bosun, and still has no idea that Sheet attached anything to his boat earlier on either. He's just aching to get on with the race.

For his part, Bosun has doubts that the plan to follow the seal will work, but thinks he'd better get the race underway while Sammy is nearby. Ignoring all normal formalities for the start of a sailing race, Bosun blows the whistle and counts down a five second warning.

"Whoops – should I have gone?" asks Rope.

"Yes, hurry up," says Sheet, passing him the Captain's cap. "As instigator of the idea, you need to wear this."

Rope is lost for words, wreathed in smiles and proudly dons the cap as Sheet leans in to push his boat off. "Fair winds to you!" she calls to him.

"Thanks." Whatever next, he thinks? What's she going on about? – *fair winds* – must be that sailing language again. And then, after a second's thought, he realises that 'fair winds' is when the wind blows you where you want to go, instead of in another direction. Cool.

Sheet gives him an extra push off, Half-Hitch barks as Rope climbs aboard. But with Painter still peering over the stern, he's having trouble getting hold of the tiller.

"Will you get out of my way?" he says to the cat. "What's got into you – why are you acting so strangely?" He hope's she'll move, but she doesn't even budge.

Halyard has been caught out by the sound of the whistle. Usually, of course, he would start the race as soon as he hears it, but today he must wait to give extra time to Rope. "Bosun, that's unfair. How long do I have now?" he asks, re-zeroing his stopwatch for his deferred start.

"Four minutes roughly."

Halyard watches Rope disappear into the distance, hot on Sammy's trail, wondering if he should have objected to the headstart idea after all, because Rope wouldn't have got so far ahead.

Sheet is pleased that Sammy is staying so close to Rope, but seeing Painter's continued fixation with the stern of the boat, she prays the cat is not being too much of a nuisance on board. All she can do is watch and hope things go well until she can get closer to Rope with some fresh bait.

Suddenly there is a loud bark from Half-Hitch which spooks both Sammy and Painter. Bosun can predict what will unfold, and while he is not worried for Painter, he does fear this might be the last they see of Sammy that day if he doesn't act quickly.

Bosun is all for Sheet's idea of dropping fresh titbits of fish into the sea as she sails around the buoys on the regatta course, in the hopes of enticing Sammy to hang around a bit longer. They had agreed earlier that it would be disastrous for Rope's plan if Sammy disappears before the end of the race, so Sheet has made this Plan B to save the day.

Halyard witnessed this private chat between Bosun and his sister earlier on, but at the time was too busy with his own last minute checks on his paddle-board to worry about what they'd been discussing. All he wants to do is win the race. But now, feeling left in the dark, he wishes he had been privy to their conversation.

Bosun is on the shore, scanning the harbour, and is relieved that he can just make out Sammy's nose as it breaks the surface of the water from time to time. The seal seems to be a fair distance from the shore and possibly heading in the wrong direction. Not all is lost…

At this moment, he decides it's time for plan B. "Sheet, if we want to stop Rope's Alternative Regatta from becoming a complete shambles, you'd better go now."

All eyes on Sammy and with the race hanging in the balance, there are now two minutes to until the "off."

"What about the countdown?"

"Needs must… *five*, four, three… just go Sheet!" says Bosun blowing a blast on the whistle.

Halyard throws his arms up into the air as he watches Sheet gaining valuable distance on him. He knows he's going to be hard pressed to catch her.

"I thought we were going together," he calls to Bosun.

"I'll explain later."

"Does that mean I should have gone?"

"Technically, yes."

In a blind panic, Halyard leaps onto the paddle-board, almost missing his footing and wobbling precariously, before he gives three mighty strokes out with the paddle. Bosun is really impressed with his determination to catch the others.

He watches as Sheet steers to where Sammy was last spotted, but knows it is anyone's guess as to where he might reappear. He's hoping Sheet's plan will do the trick and keep Sammy on Rope's scent – while giving the illusion that he is actually leading them around the race course!

Bosun laughs, seeing for the first time, the evidence of Halyard's competitive streak. It's a side of the boy he's not seen before. Halyard has a great technique – stretching his paddle arm as far out as he can get with each stroke.

Soon Halyard pulls alongside Rope.

"Have you seen Sammy?" he asked his younger brother.

"No, have you?"

Neither of them see Sammy heading off in the other direction.

Bosun hopes Sheet will activate her plan very quickly, conscious that Sammy appears to be heading towards the sandbank and shallow water – a potential danger and absolutely not ideal for the smooth running of a sailing race.

Rope is also in a dilemma, having lost sight of Sammy for over ten minutes. He's now doubting whether it was worth sharing his dream with the others after all. He's also a bit confused that he's finding himself heading back to the beach, convinced that he's going completely the wrong way. Then, from the corner of his eye, he sees the others heading in a different direction.

Hmmmm… he debates with himself whether to abandon the whole idea or carry on regardless.

But suddenly Sammy's nose reappears briefly above the surface behind him, and that makes his decision much easier. Rope is thrilled! He thinks he's now at an advantage and that it might place him back in the lead. Wonderful! He is smiling now, loving the experience again.

Up to now and after yesterday's experiences with the flags and Bosun and Sheet, Rope has been floating along in a cloud. Yes, it is true he found the flags very confusing, but the rest of the race looked so easy the way they organised it. Now he is realising that he hasn't put a second's thought into the practical elements of his plan about racing with Sammy today. His notion – silly in retrospect – was that Sammy's course would be a bit like what happened yesterday. But out on the water now, alas, it is nothing like it.

Since the start of the race, Rope senses he has been doubling back on himself a few times, just to keep Sammy in his sights. He has actually lost count of how many times, but seeing the funny side of the situation, is thankful for all the extra tacking practice it's giving him. The only thing he has yet to fathom, is what is his next move?

His brother, in his quest to win, appears to be further behind and throwing rhyme and reason overboard. Halyard reckons that if he paddles back to where he last saw Sammy, he should be able to pre-empt his next move. With all to play for in this race, Halyard feels he has the edge.

Spectating back on shore, Bosun is amused by what's unfolding on the water. The unpredictability of the seal's movements might just give Rope an advantage, he thinks. But as quickly as it came, that thought disappears as he watches Rope get distracted again by his two companions aboard. He veers off course, heading towards the shallows.

Sammy, oblivious to his role in the race, promptly swims straight past Rope and boldly surfaces close by, but neither of the boys witness this fleeting reappearance.

Sheet finds the whole thing hilarious; each time Sammy reappears her brothers' faces are a picture and she sees how differently they react. Halyard darts one way, Rope in the opposite direction and each time both lose the trail.

Bosun watches as Sammy continues to outwit the boys and – if he thinks about it honestly – himself as well.

Nobody had thought for a second, that Sammy would take a pitstop to sun himself on the sandbank…

Sheet is quickest to react and heads towards Sammy's stopping place. She is hoping that as he catches the waft from the replacement bait bucket she has onboard, he'll be hot on her trail and back into the water.

When Rope finally does catch sight of Sammy, he throws caution to the wind, pulls in sail so that the little boat powers up and sails faster and faster. His centreboard – a raiseable fin beneath the hull that acts as a balance, keeping the boat upright while sailing in deeper water – is down.

Unaware that he is no longer in deeper water, Rope skims along in fine style until – crunch – the boat hits the invisible submerged edge of the sandbank and stops dead. At the second of impact, Rope and Painter are catapulted past Half-Hitch, missing him by a whisker.

Painter shakes herself off and bolts to her old position in the stern while Rope takes a few moments to work out that has just happened. "Aah," he says and talking loudly to himself he almost expects Half-Hitch to join the conversation. The dog settles himself again as Rope takes the helm once more but then realises that they are hard aground, the centreboard stuck fast into the sediment of the bank.

Checking that the animals are all safely aboard, Rope jumps overboard, knowing that his only option to continue the race is to push the little boat back, off the sandbank and into deeper water. But he soon discovers that it's not easy and is made even harder but the extra weight of the passengers he's carrying.

Halyard feels a pang of guilt and can only watch as Rope tries to clamber back onboard. On his third attempt, he is back in position with the boat refloated. Halyard is surprised, and pleased, that Rope has managed this all on his own.

Safely back in deeper water now, their eyes are glued to the sandbank as they await Sammy's next move.

"Rope – is this bit part of your dream?" shouts Halyard.

"Maybe."

"P'rhaps you'll think twice about sharing your dreams," Halyard teases him, while being tickled pink that the wacky course that Sammy has led them has allowed him to catch up with Rope.

"Looks like our race leader's having a nap!"

"I hadn't bargained for that," admits Rope.

"Actually I think this is a great idea. I wonder what the competitors in yesterday's regatta would make of your course?"

"You two!" calls Sheet, intervening in their conversation.

"It's OK, I'll sort it." She begins to explain Plan B, but she is upwind of them both so her voice is carried away from them on the breeze, and neither hears her clearly.

"I have a message from Bosun," she tries again.

"What?"

Realising they can't hear her, she grabs the oars from the bottom of 'Come Alongside' and rows a little closer to them, taking care not to get stuck on the bank in the process. She tries again, this time louder. "HE SAID…"

"Who said?"

"Sorry – Bosun said – once you hear the next whistle, he wants us to head straight back to the shore and he plans to finish us there if you're ok with that? He had already thought that if Sammy did stop or disappear completely, this would be the fairest way to finish the race."

"Sounds fine to me."

Fine by me too, thinks Rope.

Still trying to get closer to Rope, Sheet lets out her sail to spill some wind and lose some speed, so she can get alongside him slowly and under control. As she arrives in touching distance of Rope's dinghy, Painter jumps ship into 'Come Alongside'.

Not surprised, Sheet laughs to herself. "She's caught a waft from the bucket of spare fish."

"What *bucket?*" queries Rope.

"The one I have onboard."

"Why?"

"Tell you later."

Sounds interesting, thinks Rope.

Now that they are all three within earshot, Rope looks first at Half-Hitch and then at his siblings. "Seeing as there's two of us on board my boat, do you think if I finish first, we'll be presented with two prizes?"

"Doubt it."

"Don't be silly – anyway, you're a bit premature. I'll beat you anyway," chimes in Halyard.

Sheet shrugs her shoulders, ship her oars and starts to trim the sail again in readiness for the whistle.

Lost in his own fantasies about the glittering prizes he's about to win, Rope misses the whistle. Only when he hears Halyard's paddle lunging into the water, does he look up and notice the others heading back to shore.

"Oops, better get going," Rope tells himself. Trimming his sails he heads on a direct course, sailing at speed towards the finish line which is within sight. "I got this!" he says to Half-Hitch, as they sail at the first point of sailing on a direct line to the finish with the wind behind Rope's back. He is loving it, and fully in control, for once.

With it all to play for, Halyard approaches fast and nudges ahead of Rope for a second, but then Rope catches the next gust and they are neck and neck again, neither catching Sheet who is slightly ahead.

Sheet cannot believe she is in the lead, despite contending with Painter who is dead set on stealing fish from the bucket. Shaking her head, she knows full well that Painter never misses a trick and that each time Sheet's eyes are on her sail trimming, the cat's paw is straight in the bucket for another fish.

"If I'd known you were the only one who'd benefit from the fish plan, I wouldn't have bothered," Sheet informs the cat who purrs back contentedly, whilst on the sandbank Sammy remains firmly ensconced, soaking up the sun.

A few boat lengths behind her, Halyard and Rope are still vying for second place. In a bid for more speed, Rope pulls his sail in further. Halyard, meanwhile, kneels down on his board, digging in all efforts in his last bid for a win.

Sheet is so taken up with the Painter's thieving from the bucket, that she misses that fact that she has just taken line honours, crossing the finish line first before either of her brothers. "Just one fish left," she says, then raising her head.

Within seconds, behind her, the boys cross the line in a photo finish, both shouting "I won!"

"Excuse me guys, Sheet got here before you – by a whisker," points out Bosun.

Realising she is victorious, even by such a narrow squeak, Sheet laughs and smiles at them both. Halyard is first to congratulate her.

"Well done, you won fair and square," he says, hugging his sister. "And I never thought I'd hear myself say this, but well done to you too, Rope, for convincing me to join this barmy "Alternative Regatta Day." It's been great fun! Thanks."

"Yes – thanks," Sheet responds, smiling as she picks up the bucket.

The boys watch, still no idea why she brought the bucket on board for the race. Then, turning together, they all see Sammy slide off the sandbank and back into the sea.

"He's doing a circle of honour for you, Sheet."

"He looks like he's clapping too!"

"I've heard seals are intelligent, but I never expected to see something like this."

With that, Sammy launches himself into another rotation in the water before stopping and clapping his flippers together again.

Sheet picks up the last remaining fish and flings it out to sea as far as she can in his direction.

"After all the entertainment you've provided today, I think you deserve this!"

The seal bobs his head out of the water and catches the trophy fish. Clapping his flippers one final time, he dives into the depths of the harbour and disappears.

Rope smiles. "Sammy, you might be a great pet to have, but from today's experience, you're too random for racing. I'm going to need a better idea with a different plan for next time."

"You bet," agrees Halyard.

Nodding in agreement, Sheet turns to face Bosun. "Thank you so much for all you've done – and let's not forget you saved the Alternative Regatta Day."

The boys applaud.

Bosun butts in "But hang on a minute." Nobody hears him at first, Halyard already busy proposing his gracious acceptance of joint second place. So Bosun blows the whistle.

"Hey, listen. With all Sammy's shenanigans, I think it only right to declare the race a dead heat."

"Yeah – grand idea – thanks." Halyard is delighted to hear he is a winner.

It takes a moment for the idea to sink in for Rope, but once it does, he's jumping about with excitement. "I've won my very first race – wow! – amazing!"

Sheet is content to watch them both lapping up the feeling of victory after their first Alternative Regatta.

"What a fine Alternative Regatta Day!" declares Halyard.

Bosun turns to face Rope. "The credit goes to you Rope. You showed some great initiative coming up with the idea in the first place. Well done – keep on dreaming."

There is lots of laughter and happy agreement as they all splash around in the shallows. Then, too late, they notice Half-Hitch rolling in the muddy sand, already caked again from nose to tail.

Rope leaps out of the dog's way before he starts to shake his coat, but poor Painter takes the brunt of the first shake and Sheet's legs are spattered. Both pets are now coated in mud, but to add to the mess, Sheet realises that Painter is stinking of fish after her day spent stealing from the bucket.

The boys, experienced now in pet grooming after their efforts earlier in the morning, offer to take both animals and sort them out. In fact, Halyard seems keen to shoulder the whole burden himself – possibly still feeling guilty about off-loading Half-Hitch onto his brother for selfish reasons.

"Guys – I'll take them."

"You're sure? It would be great if you did."

Rope picks up Halyard's paddle-board. "We'll sort this out for you."

"Wonderful – that'll save me a job later, *especially* as tea is waiting."

"Talking of tea, yes – Julia said it's ready when you are. I've a few checks to make before I join you back at the house," says Bosun. "Please hurry." Bosun heads off towards the Boat-Shed, leaving them to gather and sort out the boats and pets amongst themselves.

"I'm off then," and with that, Rope waves and pushes the trolley back to the Boat-Park.

Sheet takes a last look at the pets and laughs before joining Rope to help pack away the boat bits and pieces.

Halyard speaks directly to the pets. "You're a right pair – you both need a good scrub." Fortunately he had had the foresight to bring a lead for each of them, but loses his grip on Half-Hitch's collar as he tries to put a lead on Painter. Seizing the opportunity,

Half-Hitch scarpers and is last seen making for the Boat-Shed.

Seconds later, Bosun finds himself looking down into Half-Hitch's soulful eyes. "What do you think you look like? Don't bother me with your big eyes – the only thing you're getting for sure today is another good wash."

Reaching quickly for the spare lead, Bosun secures the dog and frogmarches him back to Halyard who is in the process of filling the butler sink.

"Here's another customer for you," he says to Halyard, handing over the dog.

"You shouldn't have – how kind," replies Halyard.

"Pleasure's all mine. Funny, they are impossible aren't they," adds Bosun, handing the boy a bucket and sponge for the second time that day."

"I'm getting good at this," murmurs Halyard.

"I'd call this a *déjà vu* moment," chuckles Bosun, leaving Halyard to deal with the mess.

Halyard starts by rinsing them down. Over at the boats, Rope and Sheet can see that the two animals are proving a bit of a handful, even for Halyard. So they forego their normal routine of idle chatter and get the covers on the dinghies in record time.

By now, Halyard has the sink full of lukewarm water and plenty of bubbles. He plonks Painter in first for a soak, then turns to rub Half-Hitch down to get the residual mud off his coat. The cat leaps about in the sink, trying to catch the floating bubbles, before splashing back down into the foamy water, each time soaking Halyard as she does.

Sheet arrives to help, fully expecting Half-Hitch to be submissive and subdued again, but he is bouncing around, shaking his coat each time the hose is turned on him.

"Need a hand?"

Halyard nods.

Rope takes the dog from Halyard and gives him a tummy rub – something he knows Half-Hitch likes. With no objection, Half-Hitch rolls over, as if asking for more.

"What a fine pair we have here."

Sheet wishes she could record the scene, because there are no words to convey the sense of chaos and fun they are having. It would really add to the summer holiday tales she knows she must hand-in at school when term starts again.

Soon they can all hear Rope's tummy rumbling each time food is mentioned.

"I'm off, who's joining me?" asks Sheet.

"Time for tea by the sound of my tummy."

With two immaculate pets in tow and all bundled together, they are half way through the back door when they stop dead in amazement. The spread of food on the table is incredible!

"Someone's been busy!"

"Isn't that your favourite cake, Rope?" says Sheet, spotting it amongst the fare. "Yes it is – wow, they've done us proud!"

Rope can't decide what to pick first – a chocolate muffin – angel cake? He settles for a jam sandwich and is stretching out to take one when he hears his mother's voice in his head.

"Rope, sandwiches first. Let the others sit before you decide to start."

So he stands back and waits for the others.

All turn as they hear the door.

"Bosun – look what they've done for us!"

"Well, it won't get eaten by looking at it. Tuck in!"

Chairs are drawn up to the table and the feasting starts... almost.

"Are we going to be busy tomorrow?" Sheet interrupts as they all go for their first mouthfuls.

"Are we...?"

"Yes, I think we should write individual thank you cards to Julia."

Later, after second helpings all round, the table is nearly bare. Sheet charges the glasses with orange squash and raises a toast.

"Raise our glasses!"

Rope, finishing his mouthful stands. "Yes, cheers to the team," and they all clink glasses. "Can I draw a picture to thank them instead?"

"Lovely idea!"

"I'll do it straight after tea."

Bosun leaves the table for a moment and Rope sees that he seems to be looking for something. He comes back empty handed, but then glances at the fruit bowl. "Ah – I have it."

He taps lightly on his cup. "May I have your attention for a few minutes, please?"

Instant quiet.

"We've come to that part of the day again – Prize Giving. On that note, it gives me great pleasure to witness firsthand how sportsmanlike the three of you have been today, in the running of your Alternative Regatta Day." Glancing at Rope he continues, "dreams can come true, even when the chips are down and Sammy is outwitting us all. For me it has been the best day ever! Thanks to Sammy for showing you all around the harbour, not in the manner of a traditional sailing race, but in the only way he knows – and as Rope's pet."

Rope blushes again.

"Equally, each of the pets played their part," continues Bosun, "and another big thank you must go to Sheet for having the foresight to use fish to bait Sammy from the off."

"Is that what you did, Sheet?"

"Yes, I'm afraid so Rope. At the outset, I though that fish is the only way he would stay close to you."

"Oh – and I thought it was because I adopted him as a pet that he followed me. Maybe I'll think twice about getting a seal as a pet next year."

"Don't! – we wouldn't want it any other way," exclaims Halyard.

Sheet smiles, savouring the moment.

"Hear, hear," agrees Bosun, "and now without further ado, will you all please stand and choose your prize by picking from the fruit bowl your favourite piece of fruit."

Halyard invites Rope to choose first, then Sheet.

Sheet passes her camera to Bosun. "Let's have a photo for our scrap book. Bosun would you take the shot?"

"Pleasure."

Long into the evening, bursts of laughter still echo around the Boat-House as they are still sitting in the kitchen, chatting and recounting snippets from the Alternative Regatta Day.

"What shall we do tomorrow?"

"Rope, you're impossible! Let's finish tonight first."

5

Light air day – why row when you can sail?

Unusually this morning, Rope is lounging in bed after a restful night's sleep and – surprise – no dreams. He reminisces about the silliness of yesterday's race.

"How stupid to think we could follow Sammy! – well, I suppose in a way we did."

His face is suffused with a happy smile as he looks up at the polished apples placed proudly on his shelf: his first ever trophy.

At that moment, Halyard's head appears round the bedroom door and Rope is suddenly back in the present.

"Who's stupid?" asks Halyard, and without pausing, "not up yet?" Leaving Rope no chance to reply, he adds, "There was me thinking you might fancy a walk with us, rather than staring at your apples. I promise to keep out of the mud."

Rope rolls over and faces the door. "Go on then, I'll dress and I'll be right down."

Halyard disappears downstairs to sort out Half-Hitch.

Ten minutes later they step out of the Boat-House into the heat of the morning sun. There's not a breath of wind and nobody at all on the beach.

"Wow, another perfect day!"

"If I didn't know better, I'd say it's ideal conditions to visit the seals," muses Halyard.

"Oh yes! We must do that – how exciting!"

"Hang on a second, we'll need Sheet and Bosun to agree first."

"They'll want to come for sure!"

"Hmm, I'm not sure about Sheet… she might have other ideas," says Halyard. I saw her secretly chatting with Bosun late last night and that normally means she's planning something."

"I hope not."

With the seal idea planted in his head, Rope's only thoughts now are to see where Sammy's home is. He floats off into a daydream, and begins to imagine what a seal's bedroom might look like.

"It's blue, like mine," Rope speaks his thoughts aloud.

"What's blue like yours?"

"Nothing, just a thought. Come on Halyard – we better hurry up and get back. Let's go the point and head back from there – that should be enough of a walk for Half-Hitch."

"If you say so!' replies his brother, who knows it's best to run with Rope when he has an idea.

In his excitement, Rope sets such a pace that, for the next fifteen minutes, Halyard and Half-Hitch feel as if they're on a frogmarch, struggling to keep up with him. Normally, it's the other way round.

"Will you two hurry up?" urges Rope, knowing he won't get a response.

Rope is convinced already that Sheet and Bosun are going to object to Halyard's great idea, so he has hatched a plan to persuade them.

"We must rehearse the reason that we have to go and see the seals and you are generally good at convincing them," he tells Halyard. "It will sound better coming from you – after all, it is your idea in the first place."

As he huffs and puffs along, trying to keep up with his younger brother, Halyard is now secretly wishing he'd never suggested the idea in the first place.

Rope opts to head back to the Boat-House before they even

reach the point, and Halyard is grateful for small mercies. He can already see the Boat-House door and it's a welcome sight.

Entering the Boat-House a few minutes later, the boys find Sheet has already fed Painter and is now finishing off setting the table with Bosun.

The moment Rope catches sight of his sister, he forgets that he's asked Halyard to be the spokesman and forgets even to say good morning to anyone. He launches straight in with, "Fancy a visit to the seals today? You know the conditions are perfect!"

Halyard is relieved to let Rope do the talking, having had his ear bent for the past quarter of an hour. He sits down and pours himself a fruit juice. "All yours," he says to the assembled company.

"Yes, morning to you, too. I'm fine, thanks. Can I help you?" replies Sheet in response to Rope's outburst about the seals. She passes the last cup down the table.

"Oh sorry – morning," he says, realising that in his excitement he has got completely carried away.

"That's better."

Before they are seated for breakfast, Rope pushes his luck once more. "Sheet – seriously, it will be a good bonding exercise for me and my pet. And I can practice my manoeuvres in confined spaces, too… build confidence…"

But Sheet doesn't buy his reasoning. She has her own agenda.

Rope continues, throwing in reason after reason why he should go to see the seals, completely forgetting to explain why they should all go together. During Rope's plea, Bosun winks at Sheet. Unbeknownst to Rope, the previous evening, they had already decided to go and see the seals today, but for the time being, they choose to pull his leg and make him suffer over breakfast.

"OK, that's enough. Leave it to Bosun and me to think about it, and in the meantime, I don't want to hear another thing about seals today. We'll let you know after breakfast and till then, the matter's closed."

Halyard sees the wink, and smiles back, without Rope noticing. He plays along, realising they are all up for the idea.

In fact, Sheet and Bosun have been planning this trip for weeks, but have kept it a secret from the boys, just in case they weren't blessed with the right weather conditions for the visit. They are loathe to raise hopes too early and have to disappoint.

Rope and Halyard are both over-helpful during breakfast.

"Can I get you anything?"

"Anyone like more cereal?"

"I'm fine, thanks, but perhaps Bosun might like some?" suggests Sheet.

She and Bosun lap it up!

"Rope, it might be worth you offering to clear the table…"

"It's OK guys – we were going to tell you anyway," says Sheet, a few minutes later.

"Tell us what?" they ask in unison.

"We'd originally planned to take you to the seals yesterday, but we didn't want to stop Rope's brilliant idea for the Alternative Regatta Day."

"Glad you didn't," pipes up Halyard. "It was a really great day," he continues, looking at his own prize – a fine orange, still sitting in the fruit bowl.

Bosun is next to speak. "Yes, the boats and paddle-board are launched and ready waiting. I suggest we leave shortly after breakfast."

"Yesssss!!" Rope almost shouts. "Now I'm going to be able to see Sammy's bedroom."

"Did you say 'bedroom'?"

"Yes."

"Really, Rope. You're impossible; seals don't have bedrooms."

"Why not? How d'you know?" Rope has completely convinced himself that they do.

"When you get there, you'll see why."

"Anyway, enough of that. Off you go! We can finish this conversation later. You two change and let's meet down at the jetty in ten. Will that work?"

"Yes!"

"Yes," come their quickfire replies. "It's OK by me."

"You don't need reminding, do you, to put-on your lifejackets. Before you get to the jetty, check that I see you first," adds Bosun.

Nodding eagerly, they bolt upstairs, each jostling for prime position in the bathroom. Sheet nudges in first, then Halyard playfully pushes in front of Rope.

"I'm next."

"Why am I always last?"

"Better ask yourself that question."

Rope decides best not the answer that and trots off happily to his room. As he waits his turn at the toothbrushes, he ponders that thought.

"I'm done!"

"Thanks, Halyard."

Meanwhile, both Painter and Half-Hitch are long gone by the time Rope is ready.

Halyard is first to join Bosun at the jetty.

"Anything I can help with?" he enquires.

"You can wish for a light breeze," replies Bosun, pointing at the flags. As yesterday, they are dangling languidly from the halyards. "Looking at those, I doubt the wind will come in.

You'll just have to paddle if you want to see the seals."

"OK, but haven't you forgotten one minor detail?"

"What's that?"

"You know that Rope's never rowed before?"

"Ah – good point."

"Oh well, I'm sure he'll be fine – he's picked up sailing quick enough."

Wearing his sensible hat, Bosun replies, "Let's see what happens to the wind in the next twenty minutes. I'll base my decision on what to do then."

"Sounds good… what if I show Rope how to row before we head out?"

"That's an idea – let me think about it."

This quiet conversation with Halyard, without Rope or Sheet present, gives Bosun a few minutes to gather his thoughts. He sends Halyard to fetch a spare pair of oars, just in case…

Thinking this is the most sensible approach, all that Halyard has to do now is persuade Rope of two things – to learn to row before they head off, and to take Half-Hitch too. On second thoughts, taking the dog might be a step too far. He ponders the best way to go about it.

Halyard knows he must sweeten up Rope and beg this favour. This time, he has a genuine reason for asking Rope to take the dog – he doesn't want to leave him behind and he knows how much Half-Hitch loves being on the water. And of course, as the dog can't swim, it's not a good idea to take him on a paddle-board.

He also knows the trip will be ruined if the seals so much as glimpse Half-Hitch on the paddle-board. They'll be off the banks like a bolt of lightning, straight into the depths, never to be seen again!

He emerges from the Boat-Shed with two sets of oars in his hand. Rope is a few steps behind him and sees him struggling.

"Need a hand?"

"Yes, they're a bit heavier than I thought."

Rope takes the oars but, unfamiliar with how to hold them, instantly loses control of his load and begins to wobble around. One oar shoots up in the air, the other slips out of his arms.

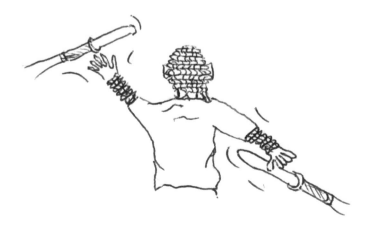

"Rope, I suggest you carry them like me, just off the middle. That'll make them easier to balance and you will be able to walk with them too."

"OK," replies Rope, looking at how Halyard and trying to copy him.

"That's better."

At this point, Halyard decides not to mention, for the moment, the reason they have the oars – nor that he is about to beg another favour for Half-Hitch.

A few seconds later, Sheet arrives and offers to take one of Rope's oars.

Halyard knows he's so lucky to have a brother and sister who are both thoughtful, and he admires the easy way Sheet explains to Rope how to hold the oars, without making it too complicated.

"Great – you have it balanced right now! Have another go with both oars now," and she passes him the second oar.

Taking the oar from her, he balances it fine and thanks her for the tip. Rope looks as if he has not a care in the world when he arrives by the jetty, placing both oars down. He's so desperate to see the seals, he's ready to do anything he's asked. The three of them wait together for the green light from Bosun before they enter the jetty, with Rope chattering ten to the dozen.

"I'm going to see the whole seal family in their home, rather than just Sammy from a distance."

"We call it a herd of seals when there's big group of them," points out Sheet.

"Really? I know you get herds of cows – but a herd of *seals*??"

"Yes, you're right. They are both herds."

At this point, Bosun waves them on.

Halyard sees his chance. "Would it make sense if today of all days, you take Half-Hitch in your little boat?" Without pausing for breath he continues, "I'm thinking that if he is hidden away with you, instead of being fully visible on my paddle-board, we might have a chance to see all the seals. We know he's harmless, but the seals won't. Whadd'ya think?"

"For sure, he can come with me," says Rope, dimly aware that it is something he might later regret having agreed to.

But before he can change his mind, Halyard wanders off to check the boats over, placing the correct size oars in both 'Come Alongside' and his brother's little boat.

Sheet also gives the boats a final check, and happy that all is in order she says, "Great, everything sorted. Oars in place. Let's go. Are we ready?"

"Not yet – need to learn to paddle."

"Ah, yes."

"Before you all head off, Halyard has kindly agreed to teach you how to row, Rope."

"Why? I'm going out in a sailing boat, not a rowing boat."

"Yes, but today is different. You can see there is very little wind and it's likely to die away. I need to be sure you know what do to if you have to row."

"OK, you've got a point there."

Rope walks over to the little boat to inspect the oars and to see how to put them in place in the rowlocks.

"They're longer than the boat!"

"Yes, they're meant to be."

"How about we tether the little boat on a long line, so Rope can get the feeling of rowing somewhere while he learns, without drifting away?" suggests Sheet.

"Great idea."

"Sheet if you can sort the tether, that'd be a great help and I'll give Rope his first briefing on rowing before he gets on the water."

Impressed by their thorough approach, Bosun offers to help. Sheet thanks him, but says they have it all sorted.

With the tether in place, Halyard knows Rope won't be able to get into too much mischief during a quick rowing lesson. He loves the way his younger brother has been showing so much enthusiasm about learning new things during their holiday. He's hoping it'll be the same today, but Rope seems more distracted than usual.

Bosun decides to watch from a distance as the two older siblings start explaining to Rope how to use the oars.

"This is more fun than I thought!" cries Rope, turning the boat in an endless circle.

"You might find it easier if you use both oars at the same time!"

"I am."

"Yes, but you need to pull them both the same way at the same time – towards you."

"Ahh."

While Halyard shouts instructions, Sheet demonstrates with actions.

"Rope, follow what Sheet's doing!"

"I am."

"Watch her again, then."

Finding it difficult to listen and watch at the same time, Rope decides to watch rather than listen. "OK, I think I've got it!"

"Yes, you look like a natural!"

"Left oar down a bit… perfect, you've got it."

After an hour of practice, Bosun wishes he had caught the whole episode on video. It would have been fun to show them in years to come how, as youngsters, they grasped the art of communication so quickly.

With the lesson and a final briefing from Bosun over, the three of them are ready to set off to see the seals.

"Remember, Rope – you follow Sheet and Halyard will follow you."

All heads nod in agreement. Half-Hitch is aboard the little boat and tucks himself in by the anchor. "Make yourself at home," Rope murmurs.

Noticing how cramped it looks on board, Sheet asks Rope if he's OK.

"Yes, we're fine. I can nudge him if I need any more space."

With a light breeze filling in, Rope opts to sail the first part of the leg to the creek, possibly aiming to pick up on rowing later. What he hadn't bargained for is that the wind is on the nose of the boat the whole way, so it's trying to blow him in the wrong direction and he needs to put in plenty of tacks. That, coupled with the lightness of the wind, makes for very slow progress. Eventually, forty minutes later, they reach the creek entrance where the seals normally hide. With little to no wind now, and no sign of a single seal, Rope is first to comment.

"Where are they, then?"

"Hiding from you, probably!" replies his brother.

"Halyard's right – if you want to see the seals, it's best if we're all really quiet and make only slow movements as we go into the creek."

"OK," Rope shouts before dropping his voice almost a whisper. "Sorry..."

Throughout their trip, the breeze has come up and completely died away again. Even Rope has felt a tiny bit bored sailing today. In fact, he might have given up earlier if it hadn't been for a game he's been playing along the way – to see if he can guess the names of as many things as possible on board his little boat. So far, he's named ten things, but is still puzzled by the funny block on the mast.

Meanwhile, Sheet and Halyard are amazed that he has made it this far under sail, knowing how tricky it is to sail in light airs. They are impressed. It would be trying for a competent sailor when wind is so light, let alone a virtual novice.

Bosun has allowed them to go slightly ahead of him, as long as they remain in position and as long as he can see them all. So far they have managed to hold position. Bosun, too, is impressed with Rope's progress and by the efforts of the older children as they wait in what are difficult conditions. He has, in the meantime, been splicing a few lines. Now is a good time for him to catch them up.

With three more bends to navigate, we'll soon be approaching the seals, thinks Sheet. Over in the little boat, Rope is mulling over some words he heard Sheet and Halyard using earlier: "a light zephyr of wind, fading". He should have asked what "zephyr" means. But he hasn't.

Rope is a few boat lengths behind Sheet. He's really pleased that he's sailed to this point, but in all the excitement of the expedition, and his game of remembering the names of the bits on board the boat, he's completely forgotten everything he's been told about rowing. He looks at Sheet with a blank expression – an expression she's seen before: what shall I do now?

Motionless, he peers up at the lank sail. Surely the wind can't just die like this? He tries gently rocking the boat, but all that happens is the sail flops from one side to the other. Determined not to give up, and still on the lookout for seals, Rope puts his head over the side and looks more closely down into the water. But all he sees is his own reflection.

"If only I'd listened to them earlier," he says to himself, annoyed that he had secretly dismissed the idea of rowing in the belief that his boat was only for sailing. The only thing he recalls is Sheet saying something about 'rowlocks first, before you row!'

A few boat lengths ahead, Sheet remembers that as she pushed Rope's boat off at the start, he'd said 'yes', but without much conviction. 'Yes' had come too easily, she muses, and she doubts he has any intention to give rowing a second thought. Instead of pushing it with him, she decides that this is a good time for Rope to figure things out for himself. When the time comes, she is happy that he'll work out by himself how to row.

Back in Rope's boat he is recalling Sheet's unconvincing smile – the one that normally suggests she 'knows best'. So he pretends everything's fine, even though his knees are firmly lodged between the oars and Half-Hitch has stretched himself right out across the oars too. An English Bulldog is quite a hefty animal and, at times, difficult to budge.

After the hectic activity of the past few days, Sheet is enjoying the tranquility of sedate rowing. It's giving her time to appreciate the peace and quiet of the creek. Even Halyard seems to be leaving a reasonable distance for once. She sees that he's slowed himself down, paddling one stroke then missing the next. He's moving at a leisurely pace.

Meanwhile, Rope's optimism is waning just like the wind. He's almost accepted that the little boat might not sail any further. Constantly pushing his legs against the thwart – the structural crosspiece that forms a seat in the boat – is tiring him out and he wishes it wasn't in his way. His slow progress is taking a toll on his patience and he fails to connect his lack of speed to the fact that there isn't actually any wind.

He remembers watching a film where the lead character shakes out pins and needles in his leg; forgetting that he's out on the water, Rope stands abruptly. He shakes his legs and the whole boat wobbles violently – not such a good idea after all. Keen to avoid falling overboard, he closes his eyes and counts to ten, holding his breath, as the motion of the boat gradually subsides. Opening his eyes, he's relieved to see that he's still dry and still onboard.

"I've not fallen into the water," he tells himself, aloud. That's the last thing he wants to do today.

Halyard has a full view of Rope's struggle to stay on board and hears him announce that he's not fallen in. "Yes, that was a close shave."

"The man in the film made it look so easy," explains Rope.

"Which man?"

"Never mind."

"By the way, Halyard, I watched you tuck the oars away. Did you check at the same time if the anchor is tied on?"

Halyard ponders the question. "Yes, why?"

"With memories of the last couple of outings and all the swimming and diving I did to retrieve the anchor last time, I'm hoping I won't need to repeat that again today."

Halyard smiles and gives him a look that says, "I get your point."

Rope looks over to where Sheet is now in earshot. "Do I need the oars to be tied on too?"

"No – just remember to keep hold of them when you paddle, though."

"Sheet, I'm thinking of anchoring first."

"I'd wait and see Rope – you should be able to row from here."

Hoping to add another helpful tip, Halyard chips in with, "Remember to pull both oars together at the same time."

Having been so excited about the seals, Rope hadn't anticipated that he would need to use the oars at all, until now.

Unable to paddle his board any slower, Halyard now breaks out of position and passes ahead of Rope. "Y'know you haven't moved in ten minutes?" he says as he overtakes.

"Haven't I? Maybe I've got weed on the rudder."

"No, it's not weed. You've no wind."

"Mmmm. What d'you want me to do about it – blow?"

"No – paddle."

Rope tries one last time to get going under sail. He wafts the sails, then pulls the tiller right across and back again. Nothing works. He's completely becalmed. There's nothing for it, anchoring won't help him. He's going to have to row.

He tries nudging the sleeping dog to move him off the oars. No response from Half-Hitch. Rope tries tugging the oars. The boat starts to rock again, but the oars remain stuck fast under the dog.

Rope's going nowhere and he's really starting to feel the size of the little boat – *small.*

Rope's mind begins to wander and he's thinking of Sammy again. How odd that since he's announced his adoption of Sammy, he's had regular sightings of the seal. But today there's not even been a glimpse of his head. When did he see him last? Rope realises that Sammy disappeared after the race yesterday, munching the trophy fish that Sheet awarded him. Thinking of trophies, he smiles again as, into his mind floats an image of his own shiny apple, back in his bedroom.

A few minutes later, still wondering what to do next, Rope recalls his first outing in the little boat; the feeling of being out on the high seas with the wind blowing past his ears. What he can't grasp at the moment is that one day there is plenty of wind and the next there's none! What a huge difference a day can make! He is suddenly beginning to realise how important wind is for sailing.

Still no seals in sight and all Rope can see is a bank of mud on both sides of the channel. He keeps saying to himself, "it's ok – they'll be round the next bend." This spurs him on, motivating him to try and solve his situation so he can get moving and see what's round the next curve. His sails continue to flop lifelessly from the mast when he suddenly realises that when Sheet and Halyard paddle and row, they make no sound at all. Perhaps I should row after all, he thinks.

After a few seconds he declares "I *am* going to row."

"Yippee," whispers Halyard, overhearing his brother's declaration.

Sheet remains silent, anxious not to spook the seals with noises. They both wait quietly for Rope as he prepares to row, knowing that seals have very sensitive hearing and that even the tiniest sound could scare them away.

Things are going well until Half-Hitch suddenly barks.

"Quick! Shush him or he'll frighten the seals," whispers Sheet urgently.

"Yes, but he's on my feet."

Half-Hitch goes quiet and Sheet decides to stand off for the time being.

Delving into his memories of this morning's rowing lesson, Rope remembers to check that the rowlocks are lodged properly into the holes in the top of the gunwale and that they are in the upright position. What next? His mind's a blank until he grabs the oars and slots them into the rowlocks. Halyard's voice replays in the back of his mind; pull on both oars equally or you'll go round in circles.

Relieved that he's getting back on the right track, Rope looks down at Half-Hitch. "You're going to have to move if you want us to see the seals."

While he coaxes the dog, Rope's grateful that the creek is a well hidden spot and there are seldom any passing visitors.

Hoping that Half-Hitch doesn't bark again and that their younger brother doesn't make any silly moves that will startle the seals. Halyard and Sheet make their way slowly and quietly towards Rope's little boat. As they get closer, Halyard signals Rope, pointing at something off the bow of his boat. Sheet is signalling in the same way, though Rope doesn't see her at first.

Finally, Rope gets the message and gives Sheet a thumbs up. Certain now that he has things sorted, and ignoring Half-Hitch still stretched across both oars, Rope stands and tugs at his oars.

"Careful as you go," whispers Sheet.

The boat rocks as Rope moves out of his sitting position. Sheet and Halyard start frantically waving and shout "No!", but Rope is far too busy to look at them as he tries to pull the oars for a second time. The boat remains stationary and the only thing that moves is Half-Hitch. Rope is thankful that he can now at least see the oars and that the dog is out of the way. But then his heart sinks – oh no – the oars are tangled in the anchor line.

Still confident that he can sort things out, Rope reverts to Plan C. Or is it Plan D? Whatever, he must get on with untangling the oars and the anchor line.

"What are you muttering about?" asks Halyard.

"Nothing really, just thinking aloud."

"Best to try and keep quiet."

Rope goes quiet and is soon drifting off in thought again. This time he's back centuries ago in the legends of history, fully appreciating the difficulty that King Arthur of the Round Table must have had when he tried to pull the sword, Excalibur, from the rock. But his current predicament snaps him back to the present, and in a huge effort to free the oars, he gives one almighty tug.

Big mistake! In a split second gravity relinquishes its control and he launches backwards, airborne, still grasping both oars. In a desperate bid to save himself from the water, he tries to lean forwards but it's futile. He continues his trajectory, out of the boat and lands with a colossal SPLASH!

Sheet and Halyard are both drenched as Rope falls into the water again. With their hands on their heads, they can't help giggling at the sight of Rope going overboard again – it's something he's getting very good at.

Sheet's first priority is to check that Half-Hitch is ok. "Brilliant, he's still on aboard, so that's one good thing."

"Yes, but he's sure to bark again."

"I'll sort it."

Halyard continues to think what he can do to help. "Rope, why don't you climb onto my paddle-board and step across from there?" he suggests.

Rope doesn't immediately reply. Good at seeing the funny side, he's holding both the oars and he's enjoying the way they help him to float without needing to tread water. He's finding it a surprisingly easy and fun experience, floating higher than normal with the help of the oars. "I wonder if seals float like this?" he muses.

Sheet heads across to retrieve Half-Hitch while Halyard paddles carefully into earshot of Rope and repeats his suggestion.

"Hang on a moment."

"Rope, if you want to have any chance at all of seeing the seals, please stop thrashing about in the water."

"Ooops, sorry."

Sheet rows past her younger brother, satisfied that Halyard is sorting out Rope, but she has to turn away. She finds the whole situation very comical and cannot keep a straight face in front of Rope.

Halyard decides to head over to Rope and let Sheet retrieve Half-Hitch from the little boat. A split second before he reaches his brother, he glimpses the seals rapidly sliding off the bank in quick succession and into the depths.

"Too late!" he calls, and rolls his eyes in disbelief.

"All that effort and nothing to show for it," says Rope, from the water.

Sheet is busy trying to quieten Half-Hitch to hear their comments. Her efforts are not working and the dog starts barking louder than ever.

"Hang on – I'm coming over!" Halyard brings his paddle-board right alongside Rope.

"I've an idea."

"Really? I hope it's better than my earlier plans!"

While all this is going on, Bosun has positioned himself at the creek entrance and is watching every move they make. So far, he is happy that the situation is under control and is content to stay on the sidelines, leaving them to sort it out themselves.

Rope is now holding the paddle-board.

"Rope, are you listening?"

"I'm all ears," comes the reply from Rope who is hoping that Sammy might just pop his head out somewhere in the vicinity to give a sense of moral support. But he doesn't.

Sheet is already busy securing 'Come Alongside' to the little boat as Rope tries to climb aboard the paddle-board without tipping Halyard into the sea. As she finishes tying the last line on, Half-Hitch leaps across without being told, and settles himself under the thwart where he normally hides. She turns her attention to securing the little boat to her stern.

Meanwhile, Halyard is skilfully stabilising the paddle-board by placing Rope's oars across the board and leaning on one side of the oars. Sheet is really impressed as she watches Rope pull himself aboard, using the other part of the oars as a counterbalance.

"Wow, that's a fine bit of manoeuvring, you two. Like your style," she quips as she approaches with the little boat in tow.

Both boys take a bow to acknowledge the compliment.

"Well of course, Rope is highly versed in the practice of getting out of the water," adds Halyard.

"Now I'm here, let's get Rope back on board his boat and see what we can salvage from our outing."

Sheet's remark prompts Rope to wonder again where Sammy might be... perhaps he's swimming underneath them? He scans the water, trying to spot him. At the same time, he watches Sheet with admiration. Not only has she sorted out their whole predicament – she is now single-handedly navigating her rowing boat 'Come Alongside' to tether them all together.

Bosun keeps watch from afar, impressed with Sheet's initiative in rafting them all up. He is also pleased with Rope's agility and balance as he moves quickly across from the paddle-board, over 'Come Alongside' and back into his own boat.

At this critical juncture, Rope feels all eyes upon him. His first priority is to make sure the mast doesn't come crashing down. It takes all his concentration to remember which cleats to undo to avert disaster. "Oh good," he mutters to himself as he carefully lets the left hand halyard off first, slowly dropping the sail into the boat with complete control. All goes well, but he does feel that he's making a real meal of the whole thing. He really wishes that one day, he'll look as relaxed on board as Sheet always does.

"Come on," he says to himself, convincing himself that he can really do it. Closing his eyes, he blocks out all distractions and tries to remember what to do next. "Come on," he repeats. And suddenly, it all comes flooding back.

Eyes wide open now, he tidies the sail away and secures the boom. He carefully locates the rowlocks into the holes in the gunwale. And now he just needs the oars, which are not on the boat with him.

"Halyard, can you do me favour?"

"Maybe – depends what it is!"

"Could you pass my oars to Sheet? – then I should be able to reach them."

"Roger," he replies.

"No – I'm Rope."

Rope's reply makes Sheet laugh. "Rope – remind me to explain about boating radio talk when we get back!"

The prospect of even more boating terminology nearly does Rope's head in. "I can't wait!" he says, mentally adding it to his long list of things to learn.

Once the oars are safely ensconced in Rope's rowlocks, the three siblings are ready for the off.

"Rope, remember to row with both hands, pulling together, then pushing together."

"Will do," he replies, wondering if he should have said 'Roger'. But as he has no radio, he decides not to.

The creek and mudflats are entirely devoid of seals. Rope scolds himself for being so pigheaded earlier on. If he had been more receptive to rowing, he might not have fallen into the water in the first place…

With his head full of his conversation with himself, he begins to stand up again. Even from a distance, Bosun hears Halyard say, "will you sit down now! We don't want a repeat performance."

Sheet's thoughts are all about Rope and what he has achieved in a relatively short time. Not only, without any previous experience, has he taken the sails down all by himself whilst out on the water; he is also about to start rowing. Yes, he's doing very well, she thinks.

She turns to release her boat from the paddle-board and at that very second, gets a perfect view of the seals returning, one by one, to bask on the mudflats. "Look," she mimes to the others, pointing at the seals.

Surprisingly, neither Half-Hitch nor Painter show the slightest interest in what's going on on the mudbank, each curled up at different ends of Sheet's boat, munching treats and unaware of the other's presence.

The next ten minutes is a chorus of "oohs" and "aaahs" as the baby seals perform a private show for Rope and his siblings. They roll right over as they slide in and out of the harbour; they seem to be playing tag, and one bonus is that a very curious youngster surfaces out of the blue next to Rope's little boat. Halyard indicates what appears to be the youngster's mother, keeping a watchful eye on him as the other seals lounge motionless, and apparently uninterested, on the mud.

Spotting Sammy, happily cuddled up next to a larger seal, possibly his mother, is the most magical moment for Rope, Sheet and Halyard. Rope feels a sense of calmness, knowing that Sammy is part of a larger family, just as he is himself. He feels blessed to have Sammy as a pet after all.

The tide is rising steadily and swallowing the mudbank by the second. As the mud shrinks, the seals begin to disappear back into the water and Sheet signals to Bosun. It's time to make their way back.

"Come on guys – time we headed back for our tea," she says, conscious of sounding a bit like Mary Poppins. "If we're lucky, Sammy might follow us all the way back." Rope hopes so, nodding his head and looking out for Sammy.

Bosun is now alongside 'Come Alongside', passing a tow line to Sheet, who secures it to her mast before passing the rest of the line on to Rope.

"Rope, if you lash it three times around your mast and pass the rest to Halyard, we can let go of the raft lines as soon as Halyard is sorted."

"Roger, will do," replies Rope and is rewarded by a smile of approval from his sister.

With all three of them securely fastened to the tow line, they follow Bosun's launch, chugging out of the creek on their way back to the shore.

Another first for Rope today – being towed. Anxious to get everything right, he follows exactly what Sheet does and so far it seems to be working well. Halyard sits down on his board, dangling his feet in the water.

"Don't fancy standing up, then?" Rope shouts to him.

"Only if you want me to fall off. No – I'll leave all the entertainment to you Rope!"

Banter over, both return to the job in hand which is to stay in line as they are fast approaching the shore. They can see Bosun preparing to release their lines.

"Bosun, if you untie my boat, I can take the others in a bit closer, if I may," suggests Sheet.

"OK, good thinking."

Sheet takes hold of the line, taking up the slack, before she rows the last bit. This way, they all make shore conveniently close to their respective launching trollies.

"Good work!"

"Yes, perfect."

"Always happy to be of service."

The boys are chattering together, reliving the best bits of the trip. "Did you see...?" and so on.

"Yes – how they rolled and slid on the mud!"

Loathe to spoil the moment, Sheet suggests they continue the chat during tea. All nod and start to help with untying tow lines. Sheet coils their ropes as neatly as when she took them onboard earlier in the day.

"Can I help?"

"Yes, if you watch, you can do the next one."

Rope is excited about yet another first, but manages to concentrate all his attention on how Sheet handles the lines. Grateful for the tip, Rope decides to retrieve Sheet's boat first, then heads over to assist Halyard.

Half-Hitch and Painter have already disembarked and

scarpered off in the direction of the Boat-House. Rope wonders why – maybe they can smell what he can smell.

"Aah, tea," he thinks, but puts that thought aside and finishes the job in hand. Single-handedly he pulls his little boat up onto its trolley without help from anyone else. He also banishes other thoughts he'd pondered earlier in the day – particularly one in which he flirted with the idea of joining a swimming club. Because he has to admit, he's spent a great deal of this holiday 'man overboard', splashing around in the harbour.

He also wonders if he's any closer to being allowed to name his little boat. Maybe, he thinks, until he looks down at the puddle of water he's standing in and relives the moment of flying through the air, oars in his hands, before submerging again in the water.

"Oh well…" he says out loud, but nobody hears him. But Rope always looks on the bright side. Falling in cooled him off, at least. He saw the seals too. He's had fun getting towed back – what a bonus – so all in all, a great day out!

Yet again his tummy rumbles. This time he listens to it and heads back to join the others for tea.

6

The mystery of the special guest

It's a few days after the trip to see the seals, and it seems to Rope that his siblings have been doing their own thing during the days since then. He's been left to his own devices, but Rope's a resourceful person and is just as happy spending time on his own, knuckling down to practise the things he's learnt.

He knows he can be a quick learner if he puts his mind to it, as long as he can avoid getting distracted. And that's the issue – the distractions. To help himself try and overcome this minor problem, he decides to make a tick-list in the shape of a boat. This will help him keep on track with the practice, he hopes.

The days pass in a blur till one morning he sees his fishing net by the front door. Hmmmm, crabbing might be fun. But no! He remembers the things on the list and decides to tackle those first.

Yesterday was a big breakthrough for Rope. He spent the morning mastering the particular rowing technique he wants to perfect. While it took a fair few hours on the water, he can now tick that one off and thinking of one more thing achieved, makes him smile.

Next on the list is anchoring practice. From experience he now knows that each time he throws the anchor overboard, he first checks to make sure it's tied on to the boat. Whilst anchored he also practises raising and lowering the sails, before stowing them neatly away.

"Wow, three ticks already. I'm steaming through this," he says to himself.

Little does he realise, as an eight year old, that everything he's doing in the way of boating is discreetly monitored by Bosun, Sheet and Halyard. They all keep an eye out so they are fully aware of what he's up to and when he needs help.

One morning he's on the way downstairs, quietly, hoping that one of his siblings might join him today. He's in a big muddle about how to tie a very important knot – a bowline – and needs some practical help. But nobody's around.

Rope's still thinking about his list and starts to eat breakfast in front of the TV. His favourite cartoon is on.

Behind him, Sheet's voice suddenly says "Oh, sorry Rope. You must have crept downstairs so quietly I didn't hear you! Do help yourself to fresh fruit salad. We've already had ours."

"If I have to!" he replies, pretending not to like fruit salad, and using a voice that he knows will wind Sheet up and get her attention.

Bosun chimes in, "Yes, after breakfast the little boat'll be ready and waiting in the creek in a special roped off area with manned safety boat cover. I've told them you'll be practising on your own."

Rope can now look forward to a day of finetuning his boat handling skills!

"Thanks for breakfast!" he calls, running upstairs for the hundredth time to read up on how to tie a bowline.

Ten minutes later he's back downstairs again.

"See you later!"

"Wait a second, says Sheet, checking that his lifejacket is properly zipped up. Satisfied that, for the fourth day in a row, he has done it perfectly by himself, she says "Excellent job! Catch you later and have a great morning! I'm sure Halyard will be out to catch you up shortly."

Feeling rather excited about the day ahead, Rope skips outside towards the creek. The morning flashes past and by the afternoon Rope is still on the water, trying his own special approach to rowing.

Meanwhile, after a leisurely lunch, Sheet and Halyard are strolling past the Boat-Shed when Bosun nabs them.

"Can you give me two minutes, please?"

Bosun wants to broach an idea with them, interested in their initial thoughts, without giving away his whole idea.

"I'd like your help with something I'm planning," he explains.

"Sure!" replies Halyard, enjoying a feeling of importance because Bosun has asked him for his opinion. "OK, spill the beans then."

"Erm…" murmurs Bosun, skirting the question. After a second he says, "well it's about a celebration that includes Rope – and you two, of course."

"If it's what I'm thinking it is, he'll be over the moon," ventures Sheet.

"Give me a reason – you haven't told us why the celebration," says Halyard whose curiosity prompts more questions.

"All in good time. I'd like it to be a bit of a surprise for you two as well."

"OK, I get it," says Halyard, winking at Bosun and recalling that he's seen Rope with a tick list in the last few days. "It must be something to do with that?" he suggests.

"Oh yes! He's ticked all bar-one," pipes up Sheet. "I think it's tying a bowline that he's struggling with." A bowline's one of the most common and useful knots in boating.

"Oh, that's why I keep hearing him muttering something about 'is it around the tree before going up the hole, or is it up the hole first?"

"If you get a chance, Halyard, could you give him a hand and show him?" suggests Sheet.

"Yes, no problem, except that you did ask me to tidy up the Boat-Shed tomorrow."

"Aah, yes. Well remembered. You might encourage Rope to help with that."

"Perfect plan – I'll mention it as soon as I see him."

"Good, that's sorted."

The two of them wait to hear more from Bosun, but while listening, they are distracted by Rope's bizarre rowing technique. He's facing forward, not backwards. What they don't realise it that Rope has decided that if he has to row, rather than sail, he wants to see where he's going and that's why he's facing forward.

Bosun tries to gain their attention. "Can you ignore Rope for a moment?"

They nod.

"First, promise me not a word to Rope about this," he continues.

"Mum's the word!"

"My lips are sealed!" adds Sheet, pulling her finger across her lips for added effect.

Rope, rowing towards the shore, notices them talking with Bosun. He sees them do a high five and leave.

"I reckon they're up to something," Rope mutters to himself, eager to find out. He rows quickly back.

Seconds later, Sheet stops in her tracks and does a U-turn. "Bosun, wait!" she calls. With her organiser's hat on, ideas tumble forth. "Can I suggest you do Rope's celebration when we muster tomorrow at tea? That will give me enough time to bake something special, while Halyard keeps Rope busy somewhere." After snatching breath she continues, "Could you put up the bunting? We do want it to be special, don't we? It's a celebration, after all!"

"Absolutely, Sheet! Great idea," replies Bosun. "I know we can count on you for coming up with a good plan."

Blushing, Sheet walks back to join Halyard.

Rope half expects Sheet, or at least Halyard, to run up to the him the moment he lands, or join him as he walks to the Boat-House, but neither do. They both carry on with that they are doing with just time for a few pleasantries. It's the kind of small-talk greeting he's heard his mother give to a distant friend.

"Hi Rope – nice rowing technique."

"Yes, it was fun!"

"Oh, good," and the conversation fades as quickly as it starts.

During the evening, Rope can't understand why everyone's so busy, except him. He had half hoped to talk about his progress before going to bed, but that doesn't happen either. And he's missing the stories he's come to expect from Sheet after tea, all about her own memories when she first started sailing.

"Night all," he says, climbing the stairs. There's no reply. His siblings are both too busy to notice him.

But while he's brushing his teeth, another possible explanation springs to mind, because Rope is unusually perceptive for an eight year old. "I should have thought of this," he tells himself in the mirror, "they deserve a holiday as well, not always to be babysitting me." He rinses his mouth. "They want time to do their own stuff."

Now he's tucked up in bed, his mind switches to what he saw as he started rowing back. What can it be that his brother, sister and Bosun are arranging? He can't get the thought out of his mind, but with no answer to the mystery, he peers up at his tick-list and feels pleased with himself. It's been another fine day on the water.

Soon afterwards, when Sheet peeks round the door, Rope is sound asleep.

"Oh dear," Sheet says to herself "he must think I'm awfully rude." She's back downstairs in a trice and asks Halyard to scribble a note for Rope. "Put something like 'if you like, let's practice knots'."

Next morning Rope wakes to find the note by his bedside. "Great!" he shouts, excited at the prospect of ticking off the last item on the tick-list. He needs to find Halyard but first, while he's trying to find his clothes, he's distracted by some lovely baking smells emanating from the kitchen directly below his bedroom.

Without bothering to dress, he goes downstairs in his PJs to find out what it's all about. But, weary from the rowing, he thuds rather than bounces, down the stairs.

"Why're you cooking?" he enquires.

Sheet's response is a little white lie. "Bosun has a special guest coming for tea and as it's Julia's day off, I offered to help with the baking." But, she thinks, it's not such a white lie after all because it really is Julia's day off and she hasn't said who the special guest is either. "Morning Rope – by the way, I had planned to say good night last night properly but by the time I got to your room, you were snoring like a trooper."

"Yes, tired after my busy day. Did you see my tick-list – *only one thing left?!*"

"Yes! That why Halyard's gone to find some suitable lines for you to practise with, so you can spend the rest of the day mastering that knot… while you help tidy the Boat-Shed."

"Oh, no sailing then?"

Sheet turns her back on him and continues with the job in hand. Rope sees that she's more interested in mixing the contents of the bowl than listening to him, but refrains from saying anything else.

"Oh, sorry Rope," says Sheet, turning to face him and realising how abrupt she must appear. "I need to crack on with these – they won't bake themselves! Halyard'll be back in a minute. Have breakfast while you wait – we've already had ours."

"It must be an important guest," comments Rope with his mouth full. "You're making all my favourite cakes and it's still really early."

"Indeed."

Bosun, seated quietly at his desk, looks over at Rope and greets him with an approving smile. "Top of the morning!"

Rope is now looking forward to his day with Halyard – apart from the tidying bits in the Boat-Shed – and tucks into his breakfast as Sheet and Bosun get on with what they're doing. But as he chews, Rope's mind is busy trying to work out who the special guest can be? He racks his brain. Who does he know who has the same favourite cakes as him? It's all adding up to a big fat zero – he can't think of anyone! Except himself…

Then Halyard walks in, stops in his tracks and says to Rope, "Glad I caught you! Bosun needs assistance to tidy the Boat-Shed. Would you like to help?" He holds up the line he has brought in for knot practice, and dangles it in front of Rope like a carrot, omitting to say that Bosun has in fact suggested Halyard asks Rope to help. "Look – I've got the line. We could combine knot practice and tidying all at the same time."

Rope tries to hide his disenchantment with the idea of tidying because he doesn't want to appear selfish, but he had really hoped for something more exciting on this last day of their holiday – like sailing in the glorious conditions he can see out of the window.

"That should tie us up till 5 o'clock," adds Halyard with a look of encouragement at his younger brother.

Enjoying the pun, Rope smiles. "OK."

"It'll be fun, I promise."

Anxious not to be cornered and asked who the special guest is, Bosun sneaks out the back door, leaving Rope chatting with Halyard.

Rope's not buying their reason for the baking, especially as both Sheet and Halyard have had permanent smiles on their faces since yesterday. He has a hunch that there's more to this than meets the eye.

Breakfast over, Rope passes the drainer to rinse his dishes and can't resist sticking his finger in the mixing bowl that Sheet has just discarded.

"That's yummy, Sheet," he proclaims in one of his nice voices. "Will I be allowed a piece of my favourite cake or is it only for the special guest?"

Sheet is keen to change the subject. "Maybe. Off you go now and change."

With the prospect of all day in the Boat-Shed, Rope goes upstairs with no urgency at all.

Back in the kitchen, Sheet and Halyard congratulate themselves. "We seem to have got him off the scent."

"Yes, but I can see by how Rope's climbed the stairs, the idea of tidying isn't going down so well."

"Yes, I get the same feeling."

"See if you can make the tidying fun. We want him to remember today for the right reasons, don't we?"

"Yes, I'll do my best," agrees Halyard, racking his brain. "Aah, yes."

Pleased to be spending the day with Halyard, Rope reappears looking more chirpy. "Come on, if we have to. Let's get this job done," he says, tugging Halyard, and with that they disappear out of the door.

To Rope's surprise, the morning flies by, possibly thanks to a constant stream of impersonations by Halyard, involving both his and Rope's favourite teacher from their school days.

The fun of remembering how to tie a bowline without pressure of any kind, makes up for the lack of time on the water. All that Bosun can hear, as he works outside, are peals of laughter coming from the Boat-Shed. Unable to resist a sneaky look, Bosun peers round the door.

"Hey, it sounds a lot of fun in here. Can I join in?" Not waiting for a response, he points to the buckets. "Wow, haven't seen that for a while."

Responding, still in character of their teacher Mrs Wort, Halyard replies, "Yes, get under the stack of sails – where else would you expect?" More gales of laughter. Realising that he's missed this silly side of Halyard, Rope is enjoying their brotherly camaraderie again.

Soon Bosun and Halyard have gone to the corner of the Boat-Shed and are nattering quietly. Rope, keen to tick off the last item on his list, takes the opportunity to sneak out of the back door with a large bucket in his hand, hoping that nobody spots him.

Engaged in chat, Bosun and Halyard have forgotten, for the time being, Sheet's instruction that Rope must not be let out of their sight, or allowed back to the Boat-House before tea time.

Figuring this might prove difficult, Sheet just manages to hide the cakes and sausage rolls as Rope opens the back door of the Boat-House.

Trying to sound calm and unflustered, she asks "So, what have you forgotten this time?"

Rope mumbles, trying to come up with a reason, all the time looking down at his shoes. Sheet knows he's lying. There's a note of surprise in his voice that is a dead give-away. Rope's a useless liar and Sheet can read him like a book.

All signs of baking have disappeared, the only clue is the lovely lingering aroma of fresh cake.

"Err, just dropped in to collect my flip-flops," Rope manages, after a few seconds pause. Sheet, thankful that Bosun has not yet put up the bunting, refrains from saying any more.

Rope places the bucket by the door and goes upstairs to tick off the last thing on the list. How to tie a bowline – done. He smiles.

Soon he's on the way back downstairs, descending the staircase in flip flops, making a deafening racket. Then he's at the door, grabbing the bucket, to head outdoors. "Just off the beach – join me, if you like!"

"Lovely idea, but I've a few things to do first. See you at five. Be prompt!"

With that, Rope bumps into Halyard who has materialised in the doorway, saying "I've been looking for you." His voice is surprised and relieved, as he throws a quick glance at Sheet who gives him the thumbs up. The secret's still safe. Rope, is fortunately too preoccupied to notice.

"Glad I've found you – you know, we've just won some brownie points from Bosun."

"Fantastic! What does that mean?" asks Rope excitedly.

"I'm sure you'll find out later," replies Halyard, stopping short, just in time, of giving the game away. Then, remembering that he doesn't know enough about the celebrations to be able to spoil the surprise anyway, he gives a sigh of relief.

"Y'know what, Halyard? I never thought tidying could be so much fun. And thanks for showing me the trick for tying a bowline. Fancy joining me at the beach?"

Halyard comes up with a silly excuse not to. "Just got to sort something out first."

"Oh, does that mean we're not going to the beach?"

"Well, why don't you go over there now and I'll join you in a moment."

"Alright – see you in a minute. I'm gonna start my sandcastle and see how big I can make it," and swinging his bucket, Rope heads away from the Boat-House with a big smile on his face.

On the path to the beach, he's too excited to think of anything else other than when will the brownie points arrive? Sheet and Halyard, meanwhile, relieved not to have blown the surprise, can now crack on with the preparations, with Rope safely out of their hair.

Out on the sand, Rope first maps the outline, then digs out heaps of sand and flings it around the outside of the hole to create side walls. After forty minutes of hard graft, he steps back to admire the replica boat he has crafted from sand, then kneels down to pat the elements of his structure firmly into place. He has lost track of time and there's no sign of the others.

Playing in his own imaginary world, he asks to come aboard. "Aye aye, permission granted," he replies in a different voice. Then he climbs down and sits astern. "Check the bilges? Check. Anchor stowed? Check." His imagination swings into overdrive as he gives the order, "Prepare to set sail – release the lines!" And in another voice, "Roger – lines released."

Rope pretends to sail off on his maiden voyage with clear passage ahead, taking in the sights of two proud sand castles straight ahead. Not wishing to hit them, he throws himself about as if he had just tacked the sandcastle boat. With his back to the port side, he has not realised that the sea water is also playing a part in his make believe adventure, as he reaches over the boat's sides. Just as he's about to tack again, he hears another voice that isn't his.

"Wow, that looks fun!"

A fellow sandcastle builder waves and smiles enthusiastically at Rope. Rope returns a hearty wave, but feeling a bit shy, he carries on with his adventure saying, "Cheers – I must crack on, I have a long passage ahead."

Still not realising he is talking aloud, nor the consequence of the rising tide astern, he continues to sail on.

"Steady as you go."

With water now around all sides of the sandcastle boat, the rising tide has thrown up another problem. The sand structure begins to crumble under the force of each ripple. Foreseeing disaster for his small craft, Rope's tone of voice changes slightly.

All sorts of thoughts spin out of his imagination and he tries to remember what he's seen people do in films when things go awry on board a big schooner. Of course, he's not on a big sailing schooner but he chides himself for not paying enough attention until, laughing, he suddenly remembers. "That's it – all hands on deck!"

And with that, Halyard appears as if by magic.

Great, even more attention, thinks Rope, who is now enjoying the game even more.

"Yes, I'm sinking!" he shouts, his toes now almost submerged in trickles of incoming seawater.

"It's not exactly the Titanic," replies Halyard.

"Yes, maybe I'm exaggerating a bit!"

Halyard springs into action and plays along with Rope. "OK, reinforce the battlements," he says and without waiting for an answer gets down on his knees and starts to repack the crumbling 'walls' of the sandcastle boat. "We'll get you off sailing in no time."

"Wonderful – thanks."

"Want to join me, building a sandcastle boat for me?"

"Why not?" and Rope flings him the bucket.

In no time, another sandcastle boat emerges from the sand, a little more primitive than Rope's first design. While Halyard puts the finishing touches to it, Rope hops back into his own.

Halyard steps back proudly. "Mine's a Pilot Launch."

"What's one of those when it's at home?"

"Ah, glad you asked… a Pilot Launch carries a Pilot out to any large ships that are coming in to a port. The pilot hops off his Launch and aboard the large ship, then guides the ship through the harbour approaches as it comes into dock. When the ships leave port to go somewhere else, the Pilot helps guide them out again."

"Wow... maybe I'll be a Pilot when I grow up?" muses Rope. Halyard giggles.

"Nothing wrong with thinking big," says Rope. Mulling that idea over he suddenly says "Let's head out to Sand Head."

"Sand Head it is."

Halyard takes on the Pilot role.

"Careful as you go."

"Aye aye, Pilot!" and they're away on another imaginary voyage.

Fortunately, and unbeknown to Rope, the tide has just turned when the others arrive so they never really get to see how much fun the two brothers were having in their makeshift sandcastle boats floating in the water.

The first thing Rope asks when he sees them arrive is "Have you brought the brownie points?" thinking he would see a plate of cookies.

"Ahh, I left them in the Boat-Shed. I'll bring them later," says Bosun, playing along.

Halyard tries to change the subject. "You missed the tide."

"Have we!"

Taking a closer look and only seeing water on one side, Sheet grasps what he means. "Oh, that would have been such fun!"

"It's OK," explains Rope "the launch pilot saved the day."

Smiling and nodding, Bosun chirps "I think you mean the Pilot on the Pilot Launch."

"Yes – that's what I said."

"If you're coming aboard, hurry up. Room for a little one."

Sheet squeezes onboard and Bosun settles himself to watch from the distance.

Watching Rope using his vivid imagination in everything he does, Halyard is reminded of his younger days and himself at eight. He savours the memory of how much fun he had acting as Rope's favourite teacher earlier in the Boat-Shed. It was worth it just to hear the laughter. He is pleased that he achieved a fun day for Rope, so that he had no time to miss sailing on his last day.

He's brought back to earth by Half-Hitch's return from the vet. The dog boldly makes himself at home on Halyard's lap and shows off his newly clipped claws. Look at me, he seems to say. He stops the sniff the sea air and gives one happy bark.

"I agree with you," Rope answers him, "a mighty fine Pilot Launch."

"Hear, hear," murmurs Sheet, fascinated by the lengths to which Rope has gone to in his imagination, listening as he points out all the features and make-believe modifications he has made to his sandcastle boat.

Bosun, too, is impressed by the knowledge of boating that Rope has absorbed in such a short time – as well as his ability to engage his brother and sister in his make-believe voyage across the sands.

He hears Rope explain to Sheet that "on my real boat I normally have the main sheet there. But I've changed it on the sandcastle boat so that it comes from the stern making it easier for me to tack. And I have space for you, too."

"Great idea!"

"Shall I pull in the main sheet for the last tack?"

"Don't be silly – it's make-believe."

Then Rope's tummy rumbles…

Without the excitement of keeping the water out, Sheet's mind begins to wander and the magic of sitting in the sand begins to recede. Hearing Rope's tummy rumbling, she prompts Halyard and Bosun to bring up the subject of tea, using her hand to imitate a pouring teapot without Rope seeing.

Taking the hint, and in his special official voice, Bosun begins. "Rope, all said and done, I think you've done a grand job creating this sandcastle boat. Well done!" He looks down, just in time to see Halyard's pilot launch get demolished by Half-Hitch's antics as he skips around the sand.

"Remind me to get you to build my pilot launch next time you're here, next year," he says to Halyard.

At that moment, a look of sadness flits across all their faces, as they realise their holiday is really drawing to its close.

Keen to keep the mood upbeat, Halyard butts in, "If I want my sandcastle boat to stand the test of time, I'll get you to design it and I'll be sure to keep Half-Hitch on a lead as well."

"Good thinking."

Just as Bosun's about to take his leave, with Sheet's teapot hand signal still in the front of his mind, he informs them all in a jovial tone, "See you in five minutes at the Boat-House. I need to get ready first to greet our special guest and collect some brownie points!" With that, he sets off to the Boat-Shed, chuckling to himself. There is but one thought in his head – I've made the right decision!

Hearing only "see you in five minutes and don't be late," Sheet jumps up and darts back to the Boat-House, where Bosun is also secretly heading.

Rope is also keen to get back, eager to collect his brownie points and to gloat about ticking the last item off his tick-list. But with that, suddenly his head is awash with confusion! To tie a bowline, does the line go first in the hole and round the tree...? Muttering to himself under his breath, he climbs out of the sandcastle boat.

Halyard notices Rope's confusion and decides to give him a few minutes to think through what he needs to do.

"I must remember – Halyard showed me three times this

morning," Rope chides himself. Not realising he has said this aloud, he's surprised when Halyard asks,

"What should you remember about this morning?"

"Oh – nothing!" Rope shakes his head in disbelief, not wanting Halyard to think he's already forgotten it all. But what Rope doesn't realise is that this is the way that every generation – for years and years and years – have learnt to tie a bowline.

In Rope's quest to remember the verse his brother taught him, he switches off, subconsciously noticing that Halyard appears to be nattering to himself a lot more than usual. A second later, he sees Sheet pop her head out of the Boat-House door. She looks both ways very quickly, then scuttles back inside. Hmmmmm, Rope is getting suspicious now!

"They're up to something!"

Halyard quickly tries to distract Rope's attention and produces a long piece of line from his pocket. "Is this what you're looking for?" he asks.

Rope takes the piece of line, and as he's about to reach the Boat-House door, the bowline rhyme comes flooding back. He goes straight in and ties a perfect knot. "Voilà! One bowline, no help!" and he takes a bow.

Perfect timing, too," adds Halyard, checking his watch. "It's time we disappear – the others'll be waiting."

"Waiting for what?"

But Halyard doesn't reply, anxious not to say too much and blow the surprise. He stands silently by, looking at his brother with I'm-not-telling eyes.

Meanwhile, Bosun is inside the Boat-House with Sheet. "It looks splendid!" he congratulates her, seeing the bunting that he was meant to have put up. Halyard ended up doing that job instead. "Rope'll be over the moon when he sees all this!"

"Yes, I think Rope might feel that all his Christmases have come at once," she replies.

The boys are at the back door now, Halyard unable to get a word in edgewise as Rope bombards him with questions. "Who is this important guest? Did I really tie the knot right? Will you tell Bosun I tied it first time?"

"Yes."

"Will I get my brownie points in a minute?"

"Yes, yes and *yes!*"

Halyard's *still* trying not to give away anything about the imminent occasion. "All Bosun instructed us to do today is to run to his schedule." And with a sleight of hand, Halyard produces a blindfold from his other pocket.

"What's that for?"

"It's Sheet's idea. You need to wear it before we can go in."

"Really!?" Rope's heart skips a beat, then starts racing. "OK, but you must promise that you'll tell Bosun as soon as you see him that I got the bowline right, all by myself."

By this point, Halyard is struggling to contain his own excitement. "Yes, yes! Will you stand still while I tie this on?"

In the meantime, inside the Boat-House, a voice says. "All we need now is for a Competent Sailor to appear."

On that prompt, Halyard opens the door and a blindfolded Rope feels his way indoors.

"Remember to tell him," he's still prompting Halyard.

"Perfect timing!" announces Sheet.

"Tell him what?"

"Before anyone says anything else, Rope's just tied a perfect bowline! There! – I've told them."

Still with the blindfold on, Rope spins himself around.

"What's going on? I can't see!"

"You're not meant to."

Rope hears laughter in the background.

"Sheet – is that you?"

No answer. Sheet tries not to move from the spot. Then Bosun says it time to take off the blindfold.

Rope stands blinking. Suddenly he sees bunting above the tea table. "Wow!"

Next he sees all his favourite treats: chocolate brownies oozing with fresh cream; a plate piled high with hot sausage rolls fresh from the oven, a pyramid of freshly cut sandwiches.

"You've really been busy!" he says, in awed tones, before asking "so why the blindfold and where's the special guest?"

No one says anything, but all eyes are on him. He tries to catch his breath as he waits for a reply. Then he looks directly at Bosun who is holding something that looks like a scroll. "Surprise! – you're the special guest, Rope."

For once, Rope is speechless. He's never before felt nervous and excited all at once. This is a totally new experience and he likes it. "Is this what getting brownie points means?"

Bosun smiles, and plays along for a few moments longer.

"Let's forget them for a second – may I continue? Before you get to open this, Rope, I'd like to say a few words."

Sensing the formality in Bosun's tone, Rope gulps and wonders what to expect next.

"Over the past few weeks, we have watched – yes, in despair at times – how you've spent many unexpected moments splashing about in the water, and how you've strived to learn to sail the little boat." Bosun goes on to recall all the great moments of the holiday and the roles played in it by Sheet, Halyard and Rope. "Yes, Half-Hitch – let's not forget you," he adds as the dog plonks himself down at Bosun's feet. Painter watches the scene from where she's safely curled in Sheet's lap.

Bosun tries to ignore Half-Hitch who is sniffing around his toes, and goes back to what he was saying. "Rope, you're a quick learner. But some credit must go to Halyard – it was his idea that you be rewarded for becoming a Competent Sailor, and without that you wouldn't have had anything specific to aim for. So thanks, Halyard."

A round of applause greets this announcement.

"And, of course, not forgetting Sheet in all this who's played a key part. She's single-handedly hit the mark on everything she's helped with: the fish episode; the equal first place, the convoy – and last but not least, her amazing baking skills. Thank you, Sheet."

Rope leans over and gives his sister a cuddle, as she blushes in the face of all this praise.

Bosun takes a quick breather, overwhelmed by the tempting aroma of hot sausage rolls and the hope that there might be a few left for his lunch tomorrow. He addresses Rope.

"Rope, finally you have reached a place that we were initially not sure you'd get to. We are all really thrilled," and with that he presents Rope with the scroll. Rope's mouth opens and remains open as he slowly opens the scroll and begins to read the words on his certificate. He takes a step back. Sheet, sensing that he's nervous, offers to read it for him. Rope nods. All eyes are again on Rope as they witness this special moment.

"It's with great pleasure that today, 21st July, we present Rope with this certificate in honour of his reaching the standards required to be a Competent Sailor."

"Thanks Bosun – if this is what brownie points are all about, I guess I'd better do some more tidying up!" exclaims Rope after a few seconds.

"Hold on a minute, you've got the wrong end of the stick," rejoins Bosun.

"…not finished yet!" cuts in Sheet. "In view of this achievement, this individual can now officially name one little boat."

"*Name a boat* – wow – is *this* what Brownie Points are all about?" says Rope aloud.

"No silly, didn't you listen to a word your sister was saying?"

This is the moment when it sinks in and Rope reads the certificate for himself, touching each word as he goes. At the bottom of the scroll, where Bosun has proudly put his signature, he sees that it has been signed in his best fountain pen which is only used on the most important business.

"Cool.... it's official, I really *am* a Competent Sailor now," he breathes.

"Yes, you are! Welcome to the world of Competent Sailors!"

"Well deserved," adds Sheet.

In the grand emotion of the event, Rope is lost for words again. Unsure how to thank them all, he reflects back over the last few days. None of it has been in vain; their secret chats, anchor practice, balancing the oars on his own, dropping the sails countless times until he could do it with his eyes shut, falling in the water – it has all been worth it after all.

"Thank you, thank you, thank you," he says, giving each a hug in turn. In all the excitement, he's forgotten about his rumbling tummy. Another first!

"Come on, let's welcome our special guest to be first to tuck into tea."

Still slow on the uptake, Rope looks round for the special guest.

"Rope – it's you!"

"Me? Really? First the certificate, then naming the boat and now first pickings at tea! What a truly brilliant day," and he sits down to the table with the widest of wide smiles.

With the pets hovering under the table waiting for treats to accidentally fall, they demolish the sandwiches. Halyard remembers his manners at the last second and lets Rope take the first sausage roll. Bosun savours the moment at the head of the table with a cup of tea and a chocolate brownie.

With his eyes bigger than his belly and his trouser waist stretched to breaking point, Rope eyes up the last sausage roll – and the last chocolate brownie. He can't decide which to have.

"Sheet, d'you fancy sharing one of these?"

"Not for me, thanks," and leaning forwards, whispers in Rope's ear, "you could always keep them for a midnight feast."

"Brilliant idea," he says.

"What's a brilliant idea?"

"Nothing," says Sheet quickly, making sure the others don't hear.

The conversation around the table sparkles, punctuated with memories of those splashy moments, bouts of laughter and plenty of "did you see me when…?" and so on.

The atmosphere in the Boat-House is electric. The whole building seems to reverberate with their laughter.

"It's not everyday we get such a fast learner," remarks Bosun presently. "So let's take full advantage of it while we can."

"Hear, hear!" and more laughter as Rope recalls the old shoe he found when he was diving for the lost anchor. Rope's cheeks ache with laughter and Halyard blushes again with embarrassment at this particular anecdote.

Bosun lets them party long into the evening. Rope is first to notice how late it is. Conscious of how much they've all done for him, he feels he should offer to clear up the tea things. Eyeing the stack of empty plates, and mindful of how Sheet always clears, he stands up and offers to take the crockery from each of the others in turn.

"Can I take that for you?" he asks each person.

"Crumbs – another first, Rope," says Halyard, standing to help him too.

"Boys, if you could load them into the dishwasher, that'd be great," Sheet adds.

But Bosun overrules her. "Leave it all be," he commands. "I'll sort it in no time. You three get ready for bed – it's been a busy day for you all. My turn now."

They race upstairs, Rope given the green light to be first into the bathroom. "Really?"

"Yes, because tomorrow we'll be back at home and back in our normal order," explains his sister.

Strains of 'It's a happy, happy day', drift from the bathroom as Rope sings and cleans his teeth at the same time. Outside, the others join in with the tune.

A little later, washed and ready for bed, the three of them pop their heads over the banister and bid Bosun a final good night.

"Night, Bosun! It's been brilliant – thanks for everything."

"Thanks – see you all in the morning," his answer floats up from the kitchen. "Has Rope cleaned his teeth properly?"

"Aye aye captain!"

Rope climbs into his bed with his secret hoard for a midnight feast. He looks at the clock. "Two hours to wait."

He turns to the window and looks out at the first stars. Smiling, he wonders whether Sammy is also in bed out among the mudbanks. His eye roams over the treasures of the day – the sausage roll, the certificate, his piece of line with the perfect bowline – and within seconds he is fast asleep, dreaming of what he's going to do next summer.

END

Is it the end?

No, or maybe the *beginning* of Rope's next adventure on the water. One noticeable shift in his thoughts are – *'boat naming'* and the *'grand launch'* next summer, then his tummy… These are just some of the chapters to follow in the pages of his next book.

Thanks

Publishing this book "Rope's off on 'The High Seas'," might have remained just a dream for me, had it not been for numerous friends including Sarah Ghinn 'Cousin Sarah' to her friends, to whom I extend my thanks. I am also grateful to my editor Annie Barletta. Adapting her technical editing skills to the world of boating like a duck to water, Annie has captured the spirit and essence of Rope's adventures at sea, true to the pace and context I have always envisaged for these stories. My acknowledgement goes to a formidable sailing friend, Franciska Bayliss, renowned and respected in the academic world for her contributions to the achievements of scholars around the globe, whose help with this book has been invaluable.

HEARTY, THANK YOU

Further Reviews

A perfect introduction to sailing and helps us all enjoy relearning the
language of pleasure of just 'messing about in boats'.

JONATHAN CLARK

Writer, yachtsman and International sailing champion

A gentle, warming and fun story of childhood
exploration in the harbour.

SARAH SPELLER

It is a fun book that captures the imagination. Delightfully
illustrated, it is a summery seaside read, full of sunshine, wind and
waves, the sounds of rigging in the wind are never far away, and the
children's joyful sounds of fun as they spend an energetic holiday
at the seaside learning how to sail.

JILL HITCHCOCK

Notes

SMBannister
Dec 2020

9 780995 542624

BOOK OF BEASTS

Compiled by Julia Middleton

Illustrated by Ken Laidlaw

GW00384507

Hippo Books
Scholastic Publications Limited
London

For Guy and Ellie

Scholastic Publications Ltd.,
10 Earlham Street, London WC2H 9RX, UK

Scholastic Inc.,
730 Broadway, New York, NY 10003, USA

Scholastic Tab Publications Ltd.,
123 Newkirk Road, Richmond Hill,
Ontario L4C 3G5, Canada

Ashton Scholastic Pty. Ltd.,
P O Box 579, Gosford, New South Wales,
Australia

Ashton Scholastic Ltd.,
165 Marua Road, Panmure, Auckland 6,
New Zealand

This collection first published by Scholastic Publications Limited, 1989

ISBN 0 590 76138 2

Made and printed by Cox & Wyman Ltd., Reading, Berks
Typeset in Plantin by AKM Associates (UK) Ltd., Southall, London

10 9 8 7 6 5 4 3 2 1

ACKNOWLEDGEMENTS

The Compiler and Publishers of this collection would like to thank the following for granting permission to reproduce copyright material:

The James Reeves Estate for THE DOZE, copyright © James Reeves; Roger Woddis for I BET YOU DIDN'T KNOW THAT, copyright © Roger Woddis; Spike Milligan for HIPPORHINOSTRICOW and SILLY OLD BABOON, copyright © Spike Milligan Productions Ltd; Anthony Thwaite for THE KANGAROO'S COFF, copyright © Anthony Thwaite and reproduced from *Allsorts 3*, edited by Ann Thwaite; J.M. Dent & Sons for HAPPINESS and MYNAH CONFUSION, copyright © Jonathan Allen; Gyles Brandreth for ANIMAL CHATTER, copyright © Gyles Brandreth; James Hurley for GREEDY DOG, copyright © James Hurley; Faber and Faber Ltd for THE NAMING OF CATS from *Old Possum's Book of Practical Cats* by T S Eliot; Oxford University Press for A NEWLY-BORN CALF, copyright © Mbuyiseni Oswald Mtshali 1971, and reproduced from *Sounds of a Cowhide Drum* by Mbuyiseni Oswald Mtshali; Watson, Little Ltd Authors' Agents for BETTER BE KIND TO THEM NOW, copyright © D J Enright and reproduced from *Rhyme Times Rhyme* published by Chatto and Windus 1974; Faber and Faber Ltd for MY BROTHER BERT, copyright © Ted Hughes and reproduced from *Meet My Folks*; Jonathan Cape Ltd for BEAR IN THERE reproduced from *A Light in the Attic* and WILD BOAR reproduced from *Where the Sidewalk Ends*, copyright © Shel Silverstein; Century Hutchinson Ltd for ANTEATER and WHITE MEN IN AFRICA, copyright © Gavin Ewart and reproduced from *The Learned Hippopotamus*; Punch Publications Ltd for I HAD A HIPPOPOTAMUS, copyright © Patrick Barrington; Richard Rieu for THE LESSER LYNX, copyright © E V Rieu; Lancaster Literature Festival for THE ELEPHANT, copyright © Debjani Chatterjee (this poem was one of the winners of the 1988 National Poetry Competition organized by the Lancaster Literature Festival); Macmillan Publishers Ltd for CHAMELEON, copyright © Alan

Brownjohn and reproduced from *Brownjohn's Beasts*; Rogers Coleridge & White Ltd for THE TIGER, copyright © Edward Lucie-Smith and reproduced from *The Kingfisher Book of Comic Verse* selected by Roger McGough and published by Kingfisher Books Ltd 1986; Gerald Duckworth & Co Ltd for THE YAK, copyright © Hilaire Belloc 1931 and reproduced from *The Bad Child's Book of Beasts*; Faber and Faber Ltd for THE CHEETAH, MY DEAREST, IS KNOWN NOT TO CHEAT, from *Rhunes and Rhymes and Tunes and Chimes*, copyright © George Barker; Penguin Books Ltd for THE OSTRICH, copyright © the Estate of Ogden Nash 1979 and reproduced from *Custard and Company* published by Kestrel Books; Trevor Dickinson for A SOUVENIR, copyright © John Kitching; Greenwillow Books, William Morrow & Co for HIPPOPOTAMUS from *Zoo Doings*, copyright © Jack Prelutsky; Methuen Children's Books Ltd for VULTURE, copyright © X J Kennedy 1975 and reproduced from *Allsorts 7*.

CONTENTS

1. I BET YOU DIDN'T KNOW THAT
Beasts from nowhere in particular

I Bet You Didn't Know That

When elephants look in a mirror
They feel so disgustingly fat,
They put on their trunks and go jogging.
            I bet you didn't know that.

1

What goes through the mind of a mackerel
Before sitting down to a sprat?
"It's true what they say – small is lovely."
                    I bet you didn't know that.

When not being dirty on telly,
The pig wipes his feet on the mat
And goes round his sty with a hoover.
                    I bet you didn't know that.

The hermit-crab, true to her nature,
Likes wearing a whelk for a hat
And showing her passion for fashion.
                    I bet you didn't know that.

The crocodile can't sing for toffee,
Except in the key of B flat,
That's why he appears to be crying.
                    I bet you didn't know that.

A mouse that is crazy for cricket
Is commonly known as a bat:
The umpire is really a vampire.
                    I bet you didn't know *that*.

Roger Woddis

The Doze

Through Dangly Woods the aimless Doze
A-dripping and a-dribbling goes.
His company no beast enjoys.
He makes a sort of hopeless noise
Between a snuffle and a snort.
His hair is neither long nor short;
His tail gets caught on briars and bushes,
As through the undergrowth he pushes.
His ears are big, but not much use.
He lives on blackberries and juice
And anything that he can get.
His feet are clumsy, wide and wet,
Slip-slopping through the bog and heather
All in the wild and weepy weather.
His young are many, and maltreat him;
But only hungry creatures eat him.
He pokes about in mossy holes,
Disturbing sleepless mice and moles,
And what he wants he never knows –
The damp, despised, and aimless Doze.

James Reeves

Beyond the Shadow of the Ship

From *The Rime of the Ancient Mariner*

Beyond the shadow of the ship,
I watch'd the water-snakes:
They moved in tracks of shining white,
And when they rear'd, the elfish light
Fell off in hoary flakes.

Within the shadow of the ship
I watch'd their rich attire:
Blue, glossy green, and velvet black,
They coil'd and swam, and every track
Was a flash of golden fire.

O happy living things! no tongue
Their beauty might declare:
A spring of love gush'd from my heart,
And I bless'd them unaware:
Sure my kind saint took pity on me,
And I bless'd them unaware.

Samuel Taylor Coleridge

As Foolish As Monkeys

As foolish as monkeys till twenty or more,
As bold as a lion till forty and four,
As cunning as foxes till threescore and ten,
We then become asses, and are no more men.

Anon

Unicorns

Unicorns do not exist;
They only think they do.
Unicorns do not exist;
They have much better things to do.

Anon

The Camel's Hump

The camel's hump is an ugly lump
  Which well you may see at the Zoo;
But uglier yet is the hump we get
  From having too little to do.

Kiddies and grown-ups too-oo-oo,
If we haven't enough to doo-oo-oo,
        We get the hump –
        Cameelious hump –
The hump that is black and blue!

We climb out of bed with a frouzly head,
  And a snarly-yarly voice.
We shiver and scowl and we grunt and we growl
  At our bath and our boots and our toys!

And there ought to be a corner for me
(And I know there is one for you)
        When we get the hump –
        Cameelious hump –
The hump that is black and blue!

The cure for this ill is not to sit still,
  Or frowst with a book by the fire;
But to take a large hoe and a shovel also,
  And dig till you gently perspire;

And then you will find that the sun and the wind,
And the Djinn of the Garden too,
      Have lifted the hump –
      The horrible hump –
The hump that is black and blue!

I get it as well as you-oo-oou,
If I haven't enough to do-oo-oo!
      We all get the hump –
      Cameelious hump –
Kiddies and grown-ups too!

Rudyard Kipling

The Dragon of Wantley

This dragon had two furious wings
One upon each shoulder,
With a sting in his tail as long as a flail
Which made him bolder and bolder.
He had long claws, and in his jaws
Four and forty teeth of iron,
With a hide as tough as any buff
Which did him round environ.

10

Have you not heard how the Trojan horse
Held seventy men in his belly?
This dragon wasn't quite so big
But very near I'll tell ye.
Devoured he poor children three
That could not with him grapple,
And at one sup he ate them up
As you would eat an apple.

All sorts of cattle this dragon did eat
Some say he ate up trees,
And that the forests sure he would
Devour by degrees.
For houses and churches were to him geese and
  turkeys
He ate all, and left none behind
But some stones, good sirs, that he
couldn't crack
Which on the hills you'll find.

Anon

The Kangaroo's Coff

*A Poem for Children Ill in Bed, Indicating
to Them the Oddities of our English
Orthography*

The eminent Professor Hoff
Kept, as a pet, a Kangaroo
Who, one March day, started a coff
That very soon turned into floo.

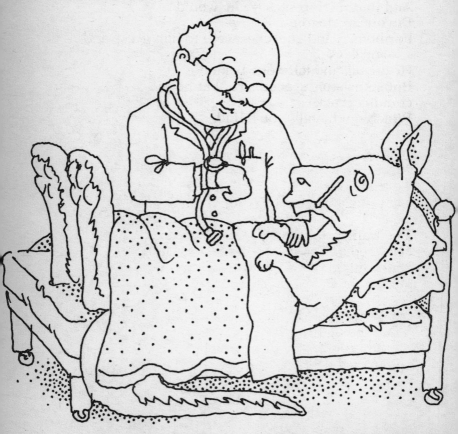

Before the flu carried him off
To hospital (still with his coff),
A messenger came panting through
The door, and saw the Kangarough.

The Kangaroo lay wanly there
Within the Prof's best big armchere,
Taking (without the power to chew)
A sip of lemonade or tew.

"O Kangaroo," the fellow said,
"I'm glad you're not already daid,
For I have here (pray do not scoff)
Some stuff for your infernal coff.

"If you will take these powdered fleas,
And just a tiny lemon squeas
Mixed with a little plain tapwater,
They'll cure you. Or at least they ater."

Prof Hoff then fixed the medicine,
Putting the fleas and lemon ine
A glass of water, which he brought
The Kangaroo as he'd been tought.

The Kangaroo drank down the draught,
Shivered and scowled – then oddly laught
And vaulted out of the armchair
Before the Prof's astonished stair –

Out of the window, in the air
Up to the highest treetop whair
He sat upon the topmost bough
And chortled down, "Look at me nough!"

13

The messenger would not receive
Reward for this, but answered, "Weive
Done our best, and that's reward
Enough, my very learned lard."

(By which he meant Professor Hoff).
As for the Kangaroo, he blew
A kiss down as the man rode off,
A cured and happy Kangarew –

As you may be, when you have read
This tale I wrote lying in bead.

Anthony Thwaite

Hipporhinostricow

Such a beast is the Hipporhinostricow
How it got so mixed up we'll never know how;
It sleeps all day, and whistles all night,
And it wears yellow socks which are far too tight.

If you laugh at the Hipporhinostricow,
You're bound to get into an awful row;
The creature is protected you see
From silly people like you and me.

Spike Milligan

The Lion and the Unicorn

The Lion and the Unicorn were fighting for the
    crown;
The Lion beat the Unicorn all round about the
    town.
Some gave them white bread, some gave them
    brown;
Some gave them plum cake, and sent them out of
    town.

Anon

One Old Oxford Ox

One old Oxford ox opening oysters.
Two toads totally tired trying to trot to Tisbury.
Three thick thumping tigers taking toast for tea.
Four finicky fishermen fishing for finny fish.
Five frippery Frenchmen foolishly fishing for frogs.
Six sportsmen shooting snipe.
Seven Severn salmon swallowing shrimps.
Eight eminent Englishmen eagerly examining
    Europe.
Nine nimble noblemen nibbling nectarines.
Ten tinkering tinkers tinkering ten tin tinder-boxes.
Eleven elephants elegantly equipped.
Twelve typographical topographers typically
    translating types.

Anon

The Mad Gardener's Song

He thought he saw an Elephant
   That practised on a fife:
He looked again and found it was
   A letter from his Wife.
"At length I realize," he said,
   "The bitterness of Life!"

He thought he saw a Buffalo
   Upon the chimney-piece:
He looked again, and found it was
   His Sister's Husband's Niece.
"Unless you leave this house," he said,
   "I'll send for the Police!"

He thought he saw a Rattlesnake
  That questioned him in Greek:
He looked again, and found it was
  The Middle of Next Week.
"The one thing I regret," he said,
  "Is that it cannot speak!"

He thought he saw a Banker's Clerk
  Descending from the bus:
He looked again, and found it was
  A Hippopotamus:
"If this should stay to dine," he said,
  "There won't be much for us!"

He thought he saw a Kangaroo
  That worked a coffee-mill:
He looked again, and found it was
  A Vegetable-Pill.
"Were I to swallow this," he said,
  "I should be very ill!"

He thought he saw a Coach-and-Four
  That stood beside his bed:
He looked again, and found it was
  A Bear without a Head.
"Poor thing," he said, "Poor silly thing!
  It's waiting to be fed!"

Lewis Carroll

The Lambton Worm

Whisht lads, haud your gobs
I'll tell yes all an awful story
Whisht lads, haud your gobs
I'll tell ye 'boot the worm.

One Sunday morning Lambton went
A-fishing in the Wear
And catched a fish upon his hook
He thowt looked varry queer
But whatna kind of fish it was
Young Lambton couldn't tell
He wouldn't fash to carry it hyem
So he hoyed it doon a well.

Now Lambton felt inclined to gan
And fight in foreign wars
He joined a troop of knights that cared
For neither wounds nor scars
And off he went to Palestine
Where queer things him befell
And varry soon forgot aboot
The queer worm doon the well.
Now this worm got fat and growed and growed
And growed an awful size
Wi' greet big head and greet big gob
And greet big goggly eyes
And when, at neets he crawled aboot
To pick up bits of news
If he felt dry upon the road
He milked a dozen coos.

This awful worm would often feed
On calves and lambs and sheep
And swellied little bairns alive
When they lay doon to sleep.
And when he'd eaten all he could
And he had had his fill
He crawled away and lapped his tail
Ten times round Penshaw Hill.

Now news of this most awful worm
And his queer gannins-on
Soon crossed the seas, got to the ears
Of brave and bold Sir John.
So hyem he come and he catched the beast
And cut it in three halves
And that soon stopped his eating bairns
And sheep and lambs and calves.

Now lads I'll haud me gob
That's all I know aboot the story
Of Sir John's clever job
Wi' the famous Lambton Worm.

Silly old baboon

There was a Baboon
Who, one afternoon,
Said, "I think I will fly to the sun."
So, with two great palms
Strapped to his arms,
He started his take-off run.

Mile after mile
He galloped in style
But never once left the ground.
"You're running too slow,"
Said a passing crow,
"Try reaching the speed of sound."

So he put on a spurt –
By God how it hurt!
The soles of his feet caught fire.
There were great clouds of steam
As he raced through a stream
But he still didn't get any higher.

Racing on through the night,
Both his knees caught alight
And smoke billowed out from his rear.
Quick to his aid
Came a fire brigade
Who chased him for over a year.

Many moons passed by.
Did Baboon ever fly?
Did he ever get to the sun?
I've just heard today
That he's well on his way!
He'll be passing through Acton at one.

P.S. Well, what do you expect from a Baboon?

Spike Milligan

23

Happiness

Enjoyment for a rat,
consists of getting fat,
Regularity of habit
is sheer pleasure for a rabbit.
Dropping things on boats
brings a pang of joy to stoats,
But heaven for a cheetah
is a Lancia three litre.

Jonathan Allen

2. I THINK I COULD TURN AND LIVE WITH ANIMALS

Beasts from home and country

Animals

I think I could turn and live with animals, they are
   so placid and self-contained;
I stand and look at them long and long.

They do not sweat and whine about their
  condition;
They do not lie awake in the dark and weep for
  their sins;

They do not make me sick discussing their duty to
  God;
Not one is dissatisfied – not one is demented with
  the mania of owning things;

Not one kneels to another, nor to his kind that
  lived thousands of years ago;
Not one is respectable or industrious over the
  whole earth.

Walt Whitman

The Cats of Kilkenny

There were two cats of Kilkenny,
Each thought there was one cat too many;
So they fought and they fit,
And they scratched and they bit,
Till, excepting their nails
And the tips of their tails,
Instead of two cats, there weren't any.

Anon

Animal Chatter

a piece of doggerel

The other morning, feeling dog-tired, I was walking
     sluggishly to school,
When I happened upon two girls I know – who
     were busy playing the fool.
They were monkeying about, having a fight –
But all that they said didn't sound quite right.
"You're batty, you are – and you're catty too."
"That's better than being ratty, you peevish shrew!"
"Don't be so waspish!" "Don't be such a pig!"
"Look who's getting cocky – your head's too big!"
"You silly goose! Let me have my say!"
"Why should I, you elephantine popinjay?!"

I stopped, I looked, I listened – and I had to laugh
Because I realised then, of course, it's never the
    cow or the calf
That behave in this bovine way.
It's mulish humans like those girls I met the other
    day.
You may think I'm too dogged, but something
    fishy's going on –
The way we beastly people speak of animals is
    definitely wrong.
Crabs are rarely crabby and mice are never
    mousey
(And I believe all lice deny that they are lousy).
You know, if I wasn't so sheepish and if I had my
    way
I'd report the English language to the RSPCA.

Gyles Brandreth

A Robin Red Breast in a Cage

From *Auguries of Innocence*

A Robin Red breast in a Cage
Puts all Heaven in a Rage.
A dove house fill'd with doves & Pigeons
Shudders Hell thro' all its regions.
A dog starv'd at his Master's Gate
Predicts the ruin of the State.
A Horse misus'd upon the Road
Calls to Heaven for Human blood.
Each outcry of the hunted Hare
A fibre of the Brain does tear.
A Skylark wounded in the wing,
A Cherubim does cease to sing.

William Blake

The Lamb

Little Lamb, who made thee?
Dost thou know who made thee?
Gave thee life and bid thee feed,
By the stream, and o'er the mead;
Gave thee clothing of delight,
Softest clothing, woolly, bright;
Gave thee such a tender voice,
Making all the vales rejoice?
Little Lamb, who made thee?
Dost thou know who made thee?

Little Lamb, I'll tell thee,
Little Lamb, I'll tell thee:
He is called by thy name,
For he calls himself a Lamb.
He is meek, and he is mild;
He became a little child.
I a child, and thou a lamb.
We are called by his name.
Little Lamb, God bless thee!
Little Lamb, God bless thee!

William Blake

Greedy Dog

This dog will eat anything.

Apple cores and bacon fat,
Milk you poured out for the cat.
He likes the string that ties the roast
And relishes hot buttered toast.
Hide your chocolates! He's a thief,
He'll even eat your handkerchief.
And if you don't like sudden shocks,
Carefully conceal your socks.
Leave some soup without a lid,
And you'll wish you never did.
When you think he must be full,
You find him gobbling bits of wool,
Orange peel or paper bags,
Dusters and old cleaning rags.

This dog will eat anything,
Except for mushrooms and cucumber.

Now what is wrong with those, I wonder?

James Hurley

The Naming of Cats

The Naming of Cats is a difficult matter,
   It isn't just one of your holiday games;
You may think at first I'm as mad as a hatter
   When I tell you, a cat must have THREE
      DIFFERENT NAMES.
First of all, there's the name that the family use
      daily,
   Such as Peter, Augustus, Alonzo or James,
Such as Victor or Jonathan, George or Bill Bailey –
   All of them sensible everyday names.
There are fancier names if you think they sound
      sweeter,
   Some for the gentlemen, some for the dames:
Such as Plato, Admetus, Electra, Demeter –
   But all of them sensible everyday names.
But I tell you, a cat needs a name that's particular,
   A name that's peculiar, and more dignified,
Else how can he keep up his tail perpendicular,
   Or spread out his whiskers, or cherish his pride?
Of names of this kind, I can give you a quorum,
   Such as Munkustrap, Quaxo, or Coricopat,
Such as Bombalurina, or else Jellylorum –
   Names that never belong to more than one cat.
But above and beyond there's still one name left
      over,
   And that is the name that you never will guess;
The name that no human research can discover –
   But THE CAT HIMSELF KNOWS, and will never
      confess.
When you notice a cat in profound meditation,
   The reason, I tell you, is always the same:

His mind is engaged in a rapt contemplation
  Of the thought, of the thought, of the thought of
    his name:
      His ineffable effable
      Effinaphineffable
Deep and inscrutable singular Name.

T. S. Eliot

A Newly-born Calf

A newly-born calf
is like oven-baked bread
steaming under a cellophane cover.
The cow cuts
the shiny coat,
as a child would
lick a toffee,
with a tongue as pink as
the sole of a foot.
The calf sways on legs
filled with jelly and custard
instead of bone and marrow;
and it totters
to suck the teats
of its mother's udder.

Oswald Mtshali

There Was a Small Maiden Named Maggie

There was a small maiden named Maggie,
Whose dog was enormous and shaggy;
   The front end of him
   Looked vicious and grim –
But the tail end was friendly and waggy.

Anon

Better Be Kind to Them Now

A squirrel is digging up the bulbs
In half the time Dad took to bury them.

A small dog is playing football
With a mob of boys. He beats them all,
Scoring goals at both ends.
A kangaroo would kick the boys as well.

Birds are so smart they can drink milk
Without removing the bottle-top.

Cats stay clean, and never have to be
Carried screaming to the bathroom.
They don't get their heads stuck in railings,
They negotiate first with their whiskers.

The gecko walks on the ceiling, and
The cheetah can outrun the Royal Scot.
The lion cures his wounds by licking them,
And the guppy has fifty babies at a go.
The cicada plays the fiddle for hours on end,
And a man-size flea could jump over St Paul's.

If ever these beasts should get together
Then we are done for, children.
I don't much fancy myself as a python's pet,
But it might come to that.

D. J. Enright

There Was an Old Man Who Said "How"

There was an Old Man who said, "How
Shall I flee from this horrible cow?
   I will sit on this stile,
   And continue to smile,
Which may soften the heart of that cow."

Edward Lear

Sheep in Winter

The sheep get up and make their many tracks
And bear a load of snow upon their backs,
And gnaw the frozen turnip to the ground
With sharp quick bite, and then go nosing round
The boy that pecks the turnips all the day
And knocks his hands to keep the cold away
And laps his legs in straw to keep them warm
And hides behind the hedges from the storm.
The sheep, as tame as dogs, go where he goes
And try to shake their fleeces from the snows,
Then leave their frozen meal and wander round
The stubble stack that stands beside the ground,
And lie all night and face the drizzling storm
And shun the hovel where they might be warm.

John Clare

Rats

From *The Pied Piper of Hamlyn*

Rats!
They fought the dogs and killed the cats,
   And bit the babies in the cradles,
And ate the cheeses out of the vats,
   And licked the soup from the cooks' own ladles,
Split open the kegs of salted sprats,
Made nests inside men's Sunday hats,
And even spoiled the women's chats
   By drowning their speaking
   With shrieking and squeaking
In fifty different sharps and flats.

Robert Browning

There Was an Old Person of Anerley

There was an Old Person of Anerley,
Whose conduct was strange and unmannerly:
   He rushed down the Strand,
   With a Pig in each hand,
But returned in the evening to Anerley.

Edward Lear

My Brother Bert

Pets are the Hobby of my brother Bert.
He used to go to school with a Mouse in his shirt.

His Hobby it grew, as some hobbies will,
And grew and GREW and **GREW** until –

Oh don't breathe a word, pretend you haven't
      heard.
A simply appalling thing has occurred –

The very thought makes me iller and iller:
Bert's brought home a gigantic Gorilla!

If you think that's really not such a scare,
What if it quarrels with his Grizzly Bear?

You still think you could keep your head?
What if the Lion from under the bed

And the four Ostriches that deposit
Their football eggs in his bedroom closet

And the Aardvark out of his bottom drawer
All danced out and joined in the Roar?

What if the Pangolins were to caper
Out of their nests behind the wallpaper?

With the fifty sorts of Bats
That hang on his hatstand like old hats,

And out of a shoebox the excitable Platypus
Along with the Ocelot or Jungle-Cattypus?

The Wombat, the Dingo, the Gecko, the Grampus –
How they would shake the house with their
    Rumpus!

Not to forget the Bandicoot
Who would certainly peer from his battered old
    boot.

Why it would be a dreadful day,
And what Oh what would the neighbours say!

Ted Hughes

3. IN THE FORESTS OF THE NIGHT

Beasts from the wild

The Tyger

Tyger! Tyger! burning bright
In the forests of the night,
What immortal hand or eye
Could frame thy fearful symmetry?

In what distant deeps or skies
Burnt the fire of thine eyes?
On what wings dare he aspire?
What the hand dare seize the fire?

And what shoulder, and what art,
Could twist the sinews of thy heart?
And when thy heart began to beat,
What dread hand? And what dread feet?

What the hammer? What the chain?
In what furnace was thy brain?
What the anvil? What dread grasp
Dare its deadly terrors clasp?

When the stars threw down their spears,
And water'd heaven with their tears,
Did he smile his work to see?
Did he who made the Lamb make thee?

Tyger! Tyger! burning bright
In the forests of the night,
What immortal hand or eye
Dare frame thy fearful symmetry?

William Blake

Bear in there

There's a Polar Bear
In our Frigidaire –
He likes it 'cause it's cold in there.
With his seat in the meat
And his face in the fish
And his big hairy paws
In the butter dish,
He's nibbling the noodles,
He's munching the rice,
He's slurping the soda,
He's licking the ice.
And he lets out a roar
If you open the door.
And it gives me a scare
To know he's in there –
That Polary Bear
In our Fridgitydaire.

Shel Silverstein

48

The Anteater

The Anteater
Isn't a small or a scant eater.
To keep going and in the pink
It has to eat many more ants than you might think!
To get to be really fit – and stay that way –
It has to eat hundreds of thousands a day!

Gavin Ewart

The Blind Men and the Elephant

It was six men of Hindostan,
To learning much inclined,
Who went to see the elephant,
(Though all of them were blind);
That each by observation
Might satisfy his mind.

The first approached the elephant,
And happening to fall
Against his broad and sturdy side,
At once began to bawl,
"Bless me, it seems the elephant
Is very like a wall."

The second, feeling of his tusk,
Cried, "Ho! What have we here
So very round and smooth and sharp?
To me 'tis mighty clear
This wonder of an elephant
Is very like a spear."

The third approached the animal,
And happening to take
The squirming trunk within his hands,
Then boldly up and spake;
"I see" quoth he, "the elephant
Is very like a snake."

The fourth stretched out his eager hand
And felt about the knee,
"What most this mighty beast is like
Is mighty plain," quoth he;
"'Tis clear enough the elephant
Is very like a tree."

The fifth who chanced to touch the ear
Said, "Even the blindest man
Can tell what this resembles most;
Deny the fact who can,
This marvel of an elephant
Is very like a fan."

The sixth no sooner had begun
About the beast to grope
Than, seizing on the swinging tail
That fell within his scope,
"I see," cried he, "The elephant
Is very like a rope."

And so these men of Hindostan
Disputed loud and long,
Each of his own opinion
Exceeding stiff and strong,
Though each was partly in the right,
And all were in the wrong!

John Godfrey Saxe

Chameleon

I can think sharply
and I can change:
My colours cover a considerable range.

I can be some mud by
an estuary,
I can be a patch on the bark of a tree.

I can be green grass
or a little thin stone
– or if I really want to be left alone,

I can be a shadow . . . .
What I am on your
multi-coloured bedspread, I am not quite sure.

Alan Brownjohn

There Was a Young Lady of Niger

There was a young lady of Niger
Who smiled as she rode on a tiger;
   They returned from the ride
    With the lady inside,
And the smile on the face of the tiger.

Anon

The Lesser Lynx

The laughter of the lesser Lynx
   Is often insincere:
It pays to be polite, he thinks,
   If Royalty is near.

So when the Lion steals his food
   Or kicks him from behind,
He smiles, of course – but oh, the rude
   Remarks that cross his mind!

E.V. Rieu

The Elephant

Elephants were not her cup of tea –
they were mammoth and boring,
immobile, they turned no somersaults.
Gaiety and the antics of monkeys
and insulting parakeets,
blinking and chattering,
offered her the warmth of fur and vivid feathers.
Elephants were distant, tusked and ominous.
Powerful and towering over children,
their long memories and wisdom
placed them in a different zoo for adults.

"But this is an Indian elephant,"
her father said. "It is homesick
and will cheer up to see an Indian girl
in this wet, cold, foreign land."
So she tore away from the noisy cages
and allowed herself to be slowly led
to greet her majestic compatriot.
She avoided those massive tree trunk legs
And looked straight up at the eyes.
A storehouse of sorrow was locked in its brain.
Tentative, she reached out a hand and patted
the incredible trunk stretched out to her.

Debjani Chatterjee

The Tiger

A tiger going for a stroll
Met an old man and ate him whole.

The old man shouted, and he thumped.
The tiger's stomach churned and bumped.

The other tigers said: "Now really,
We hear your breakfast much too clearly."

The moral is, he should have chewed.
It does no good to bolt one's food.

Edward Lucie-Smith

A Cheerful Old Bear at the Zoo

A cheerful old bear at the zoo
Could always find something to do.
   When it bored him to go
   On a walk to and fro,
He reversed it, and walked fro and to.

Anon

I Had a Hippopotamus

I had a hippopotamus; I kept him in a shed
And fed him upon vitamins and vegetable bread;
I made him my companion on many cheery walks,
And had his portrait done by a celebrity in chalks.

His charming eccentricities were known on every
    side,
The creature's popularity was wonderfully wide;
He frolicked with the Rector in a dozen friendly
    tussles,
Who could not but remark upon his
    hippopotamuscles.

If he should be afflicted by depression or the
      dumps,
By hippopotameasles or the hippopotamumps,
I never knew a particle of peace till it was plain
He was hippopotamasticating properly again.

I had a hippopotamus; I loved him as a friend;
But beautiful relationships are bound to have an
      end;
Time takes, alas! our joys from us and robs us of
      our blisses;
My hippopotamus turned out a hippopotamissis.

My housekeeper regarded him with jaundice in her
      eye;
She did not want a colony of hippopotami;
She borrowed a machine-gun from her soldier-
      nephew, Percy,
And showed my hippopotamus no
      hippopotamercy.

My house now lacks the glamour that the
      charming creature gave,
The garage where I kept him is as silent as the
      grave;
No longer he displays among the motor-tyres and
      spanners
His hippopotamastery of hippopotamanners.

No longer now he gambols in the orchards in the
    spring;
No longer do I lead him through the village on a
    string;
No longer in the mornings does the neighbourhood
    rejoice
To his hippopotamusically-modulated voice.

I had a hippopotamus; but nothing upon earth
Is constant in its happiness or lasting in its mirth;
No joy that life can give me can be strong enough
    to smother
My sorrow for that might-have-been-a-
    hippopotamother.

Patrick Barrington

The Yak

As a friend to the children commend me the Yak.
  You will find it exactly the thing:
It will carry and fetch, you can ride on its back,
  Or lead it about with a string.

The Tartar who lives on the plains of Tibet
  (A desolate region of snow)
Has for centuries made it a nursery pet,
  And surely the Tartar should know!

Then tell your papa where the Yak can be got,
  And if he is awfully rich
He will buy you the creature – or else he will not.
  (I cannot be positive which.)

Hilaire Belloc

White Men in Africa

White men in Africa,
Puffing at their pipes,
Think the Zebra's a white horse
With black stripes.

Black men in Africa,
With pipes of different types,
Know the Zebra's a black horse
With white stripes.

Gavin Ewart

The Cheetah, my Dearest, is Known not to Cheat

The cheetah, my dearest, is known not to cheat;
the tiger possesses no tie;
the horse-fly, of course, was never a horse;
the lion will not tell a lie.

The turkey, though perky, was never a Turk;
nor the monkey ever a monk;
the mandrel, though like one, was never a man,
but some men are like him, when drunk.

The springbok, dear thing, was not born in the
    Spring;
the walrus will not build a wall.
No badger is bad; no adder can add.
There is no truth in these things at all.

George Barker

Wild Boar

If you tell me the wild boar
Has twenty teeth, I'll say, "Why shore."
Or say that he has thirty-three,
That number's quite all right with me.
Or scream that he has ninety-nine,
I'll never say that you are lyin',
For the number of teeth
In a wild boar's mouth
Is a subject I'm glad
I know nothing abouth.

Shel Silverstein

4. THE WRINKLED SEA BENEATH HIM CRAWLS

Beasts from sky and water

The Eagle

He clasps the crag with crookèd hands:
Close to the sun in lonely lands,
Ringed with the azure world, he stands.

The wrinkled sea beneath him crawls;
He watches from his mountain walls,
And like a thunderbolt he falls.

Alfred, Lord Tennyson

The Ostrich

The ostrich roams the great Sahara,
Its mouth is wide, its neck is narra.
It has such long and lofty legs,
I'm glad it sits to lay its eggs.

Ogden Nash

A Souvenir

On my Auntie Mabel's mantelpiece
There sits a seal. Not live and real
Of course, but tiny, dead and real.
Know what I mean? It's made of seal;
Dead thing, but true to life in each detail.

I wonder how a seal must think
(If think it can) or feel at brink
Of sea to hear the culling call
Of man to man as men wade in
To beat with staves this solid flesh
(Still frail) to make a souvenir of Canada
That sits on Auntie Mabel's mantelpiece.

John Kitching

69

The Lobster Quadrille

"Will you walk a little faster?" said a whiting to a
    snail,
"There's a porpoise close behind us, and he's
    treading on my tail.
See how eagerly the lobsters and the turtles all
    advance!
They are waiting on the shingle – will you come
    and join the dance?
  Will you, won't you, will you, won't you, will you
    join the dance?
  Will you, won't you, will you, won't you, won't
    you join the dance?

"You can really have no notion how delightful it
    will be
When they take us up and throw us, with the
    lobsters, out to sea!"
But the snail replied "Too far, too far!" and gave a
    look askance –

Said he thanked the whiting kindly, but he would
   not join the dance.
  Would not, could not, would not, could not,
    would not join the dance.
  Would not, could not, would not, could not,
    could not join the dance.

"What matters it how far we go?" his scaly friend
   replied.
"There is another shore, you know, upon the other
    side.
The further off from England the nearer is to
    France –
Then turn not pale, beloved snail, but come and
   join the dance.
  Will you, won't you, will you, won't you, will you
    join the dance?
  Will you, won't you, will you, won't you, won't
    you join the dance?"

Lewis Carroll

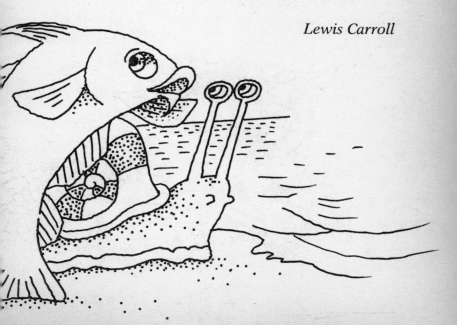

The Duck and the Kangaroo

Said the Duck to the Kangaroo,
  "Good gracious! how you hop!
Over the fields and the water too,
  As if you never would stop!
My life is a bore in this nasty pond,
And I long to go out in the world beyond!
  I wish I could hop like you!"
  Said the Duck to the Kangaroo.

"Please give me a ride on your back!"
  Said the Duck to the Kangaroo.
"I would sit quite still, and say nothing but 'Quack',
  The whole of the long day through!
And we'd go to the Dee, and the Jelly Bo Lee,
Over the land, and over the sea; –
  Please take me a ride! O do!"
  Said the Duck to the Kangaroo.

Said the Kangaroo to the Duck,
  "This requires some little reflection;
Perhaps on the whole it might bring me luck,
  And there seems but one objection,
Which is, if you'll let me speak so bold,
Your feet are unpleasantly wet and cold,
  And would probably give me the roo-
  Matiz!" said the Kangaroo.

Said the Duck, "As I sate on the rocks,
  I have thought over that completely,
And I bought four pairs of worsted socks
  Which fit my web-feet neatly.
And to keep out the cold I've bought a cloak,
And every day a cigar I'll smoke,
  All to follow my own dear true
  Love of a Kangaroo!"

Said the Kangaroo, "I'm ready!
  All in the moonlight pale;
But to balance me well, dear Duck, sit steady!
  And quite at the end of my tail!"
So away they went with a hop and a bound,
And they hopped the whole world three times
      round;
  And who so happy, – O who,
  As the Duck and the Kangaroo?

                                    Edward Lear

Natural History

The common cormorant or shag
Lays eggs inside a paper bag
The reason you will see no doubt
Is to keep the lightning out
But what these unobservant birds
Have never noticed is that herds
Of wandering bears may come with buns
And steal the bags to hold the crumbs.

Christopher Isherwood

There Was an Old Man with a Beard

There was an Old Man with a beard,
Who said, "It is just as I feared! –
   Two Owls and a Hen,
   Four Larks and a Wren,
Have all built their nests in my beard!"

Edward Lear

At Whipsnade Zoo

By a large round pond at Whipsnade Zoo
A tiger lives, and a duck lives too.

The tiger is dreaming of hunting and slaughter,
Duck pushes his luck and comes out of the water.

He waddles up close, has he taken a bet?
Tiger stretches his claws but he doesn't spring yet.

Instead, he stands languidly . . . advances a pace,
The duck sets off hurriedly (with somewhat less
        grace).

The tiger steps swiftly; the duck's waddles quicken
And just at the moment when duck should be
        stricken

He slips off the land and slides onto the pool –
The tiger starts drinking to show he's no fool,

Then returns to his previous somnolent pose
As the ripple surrounding the scheming duck
        grows.

A few minutes later the tiger lies still,
His eyes blinking gently, he dreams of the kill.

The duck, tired of swimming, makes another
        advance:
He's asking his "partner" to join in the dance.

But the tiger's not hungry and the duck's just a
    tease.
Still . . . as soon as the tiger's mouth opens, he flees.

By a large round pond at Whipsnade Zoo
A duck lives on, and a tiger too.

Julia Middleton

Mynah Confusion

The diner heard the mynah bird,
the mynah heard the diner,
    and the word the diner heard
the mynah say was so absurd
that when the mynah heard the diner say
    the word he said the mynah said,
the mynah realised the diner
    ·hadn't heard at all.

Jonathan Allen

The Hippopotamus

The huge hippopotamus hasn't a hair
on the back of his wrinkly hide;
he carries the bulk of his prominent hulk
rather loosely assembled inside.

The huge hippopotamus lives without care
at a slow philosophical pace,
as he wades in the mud with a thump and a thud
and a permanent grin on his face.

Jack Prelutsky

How Doth the Little Crocodile

How doth the little crocodile
  Improve his shining tail,
And pour the waters of the Nile
  On every golden scale!

How cheerfully he seems to grin,
  How neatly spreads his claws,
And welcomes little fishes in,
  With gently smiling jaws!

Lewis Carroll

The Owl and the Pussy-Cat

The Owl and the Pussy-Cat went to sea
  In a beautiful pea-green boat,
They took some honey, and plenty of money,
  Wrapped up in a five-pound note.
The Owl looked up to the stars above,
  And sang to a small guitar,
"O lovely Pussy! O Pussy, my love,
  What a beautiful Pussy you are,
    You are,
    You are!
  What a beautiful Pussy you are!"

Pussy said to the Owl, "You elegant fowl!
    How charmingly sweet you sing!
O let us be married! too long we have tarried:
    But what shall we do for a ring?"
They sailed away, for a year and a day,
    To the land where the Bong-tree grows,
And there in a wood a Piggy-wig stood,
    With a ring at the end of his nose,
        His nose,
        His nose,
With a ring at the end of his nose.

"Dear Pig, are you willing to sell for one shilling,
    Your ring?" Said the Piggy, "I will."
So they took it away, and were married next day
    By the turkey who lives on the hill.
They dined on mince, and slices of quince,
    Which they ate with a runcible spoon;
And hand in hand, on the edge of the sand,
    They danced by the light of the moon,
        The moon,
        The moon,
They danced by the light of the moon.

Edward Lear

Vulture

The vulture's very like a sack
Set down and left there drooping.
His crooked neck and creaky beak
Look badly bent from stooping
Down to the ground to eat dead cows
So they won't go to waste,
Thus making up in usefulness
For what he lacks in taste.

X.J. Kennedy

Index of beasts

Index of titles

Index of poets